THE BILLIONAIRE'S BABY ARRANGEMENT

KRISTA LAKES

ZIRCONIA PUBLISHING, INC.

The Billionaire's Baby Arrangement

From New York Times bestselling author Krista Lakes comes a sexy standalone novel about a billionaire and the indecent proposal he gives the local barista.

Billionaire CEO Jackson Weathers needs a family for a PR boost, and I've signed a contract agreeing to give him one. A doting girlfriend in public. A wedding ceremony to invite all the socialites to. And finally, a baby for him to parade around, to show he's really a wholesome, down-to-Earth man.

I've tried to remain cynical about it. He's going to make all my dreams come true. So what if it's supposed to be a loveless marriage?

Only, his tenderness in private has me hooked. The way he kisses me drives me wild. When we make love, I lose myself to him. His body feels like it was meant to be on top of mine, like we fit together like two puzzle pieces. I can't help but begin to fall for him.

I can't tell him, or I risk losing everything. And nobody else can find out about our little "arrangement" or it will destroy his reputation. Still, I feel like I have to know how he feels, before the marriage, before the baby, before I give my entire life over to him.

Is it still just pretend?

∼

"I was wondering when you were going to get home." Her hand went to the silky collar of her robe and she tugged on it gently to reveal just a hint of smooth skin underneath. She liked that he swallowed hard and stared.

"Work went long," he said, his eyes still glued to the bare skin of her chest. She let the robe open just a little more. "If I had known this was waiting for me, I would have been home hours ago."

She grinned and stood from the couch. She flipped off the light, letting just the pale glow from the city lights fill the room. With a grin, she undid the ties to the robe and let the fabric slide to the floor. The pale silk pooled around her ankles as she stood naked before him in the pale twilight. She knew the lack of light would hide her flaws.

His reaction made all the waiting worth it. His eyes dilated, his mouth opened, and she could see the growing bulge in his pants. She rather liked having this effect on him. She knew that he found her beautiful. She knew that he found her sexually attractive, but to see his actual reaction would never get old.

She felt like a goddess when he looked at her like that.

He reached out a finger and caressed the arch of her collarbone, his finger then tracing the curve of her shoulder down her arm. Goosebumps popped out along her skin, but it wasn't from cold. It was pure desire at being touched. His fingers caught the swell of her breast, skimming along the curve and barely touching her.

Her nipples hardened in front of his eyes. Hunger blossomed on his face as he cupped her breast in his warm hand, his thumb rubbing against the hard nipple. Jackson's pupils nearly took over the green of his eyes.

She took a step forward, threading her hand over his shoulder and into his hair as she pressed her naked body against his suit. She could feel the warm, hard spot at her groin as she leaned in, drawing his lips to hers.

He tasted so good. Every time he kissed her he tasted better. His mouth opened and his tongue quested into her waiting mouth, tangling with her tongue. His hand was still on her breast, playing with the nipple while the other hand went to her hip and pulled her further into him.

She pulled back, gazing up at him through long lashes and grinning. She rocked her naked hips into his, feeling him harden further. With the hand not around his neck, she grabbed his tie, fisting the silk, and pulled him in for another kiss.

This kiss was urgent. She wanted to feel him inside of her. She wanted his hard length to fill her. Heat was building in her core and he was the only one who could put it out.

He kissed her, letting her be in control for a moment. She smiled as she kissed him, enjoying the idea that the naked woman was the one in control of the clothed, powerful businessman.

He groaned, and his hand tightened on her hip. She wasn't in quite as much control as he let her think. He was bigger and stronger. His hip thrust into her, letting her know that he was going to fuck her the moment he had the chance.

And she was very okay with that.

mma

"Welcome to Coffee Shack, Mrs. Johnson." Emma greeted her next customer with a smile. "Your usual?"

The woman in a suit nodded, barely looking up from her phone. That was typical here. The coffee shop was located on the first floor of a downtown skyscraper with all sorts of important businesses filling the offices upstairs. W&W BabyCo held most of the floors, but there was also an internet company and a well respected law firm in the building. Everyone who came for coffee was usually busy with some sort of important work.

"Grande triple mocha with almond milk," Emma called out, taking Mrs. Johnson's money. Emma handed the card back with a smile that Mrs. Johnson hardly acknowledged before stepping to the side for the next person to order. Emma grinned as she realized it was her best friend.

"Hi, Grace," Emma said warmly to her friend. "Hi,

Sammy," she said, waving to the little boy on Grace's hip. "What can I get you?"

"I need an extra shot today, Emma," Grace told her, hiking the baby up higher on her hip. "Sam here is working on a new tooth and decided that he didn't want to sleep last night because of it."

"Oh, I'm so sorry to hear that," Emma replied, writing the order on a paper cup. She added a plus one to the shots. "It's a dollar extra for the shot. My poor Sammy."

Grace reached into her pocket and rummaged around before shaking her head and sighing. "Never mind. Take the shot off. I don't have any extra today."

Emma glanced over at her busy boss and then back to her customer. "The extra shot's on me, then," Emma whispered.

"You are a saint," Grace told her, handing Emma her coffee card. The look of relief and gratitude coming from the young mother was more than enough payment for Emma. "I'm just so tired today. I'd forget my head if it wasn't attached. I thought I had an extra dollar in my pocket."

"It's my pleasure. Can he have a C-O-O-K-I-E? We have samples today," Emma said, spelling out the word so she wouldn't get Sam in trouble.

"He'd love some cookie," Grace told her with a smile. "It'll feel good on his teeth."

Emma went to the cookie display and picked out the most colorful one. She carefully wrapped it up in a bag and handed it to Grace.

"Are we still on for me babysitting tonight?" Emma asked.

"Yes!" Grace replied emphatically. "I've been looking forward to date night for the whole month now. You're sure you're okay with Sam? This teething stage is terrible."

"Sam and I are buddies," Emma assured her. She grinned at the one-year old boy. "Aren't we?"

"Ahmm," Sam replied with a nod, making Emma grin. She

loved that little boy with her whole heart. She had from the moment she'd met him.

"Okay, I'll see you in a little bit," Grace said, stepping to the side. There wasn't another customer behind her. "Thank you so much, Emma. You're a lifesaver."

"I'm going on break in a few minutes and I'll come over and get some Sammy hugs," Emma replied. Grace grinned, knowing that meant she'd get to drink her coffee in peace while Emma distracted and played with the little boy.

Emma turned back to the job at hand. Walking up to the counter was her favorite customer. She felt her stomach flutter and she made sure her hat was on straight. This was usually the best part of her entire day.

Mr. Jackson Weathers owned W&W BabyCo. She knew he had to be worth billions, yet he always came and ordered coffee from her on his way up to his office. She took it as a compliment, given that most of his senior staff simply had it delivered to the top floor.

"Good morning, Mr. Weathers," Emma greeted him warmly. "How are you today?"

"I'm great," he assured her, flashing his trademark smile. The man was gorgeous. Her knees went a little weak. She couldn't help it. The man was absurdly good looking. He was tall, with strong shoulders that told her he worked out. She'd seen him run in wearing gym clothes and knew that he really did have a great physique under his suit. There was no shoulder padding accentuating his body.

His hair looked like a Disney artist drew it every morning. The medium blond hair was always perfectly styled and just tousled enough to make her want to run her fingers through it. Bright green eyes sparkled at her when he smiled, and that was her real weakness. That sparkle.

He was all charm and sparkle.

He was also the most notorious playboy and flirt

she'd ever met. She'd seen way too many gorgeous women on his arm to even think she ever had a chance. He liked to flirt with her, but she knew it was just for fun.

He would never seriously date a nobody like her.

"Your usual?" she asked him, smiling back at him. Even though he was so out of her league they were playing different sports, she could still enjoy their morning conversation.

"Yes, please," he replied.

"One grande Americano, extra shot, two pumps cinnamon dolce," she called out.

"How do you remember everyone's order?" he asked her, looking impressed. He leaned against the counter. Every movement was easy and meant to attract her.

She shrugged. "How do you remember your date's names? Practice."

He laughed. "Ouch."

She shrugged. "I call it like I see it," she teased him.

He grinned. "Maybe I should take you out to dinner. I think I can remember your name. Betsy? Olga? Helga. Definitely Helga."

"Me?" She chuckled. They had this conversation at least once a month. "I thought that you were currently working your way through the New York Ballet. I'm afraid I am not currently a member."

"Could have fooled me," he told her, flashing her that grin again. Her heart fluttered. Flirting with a professional flirt was fun.

"Do you want a cookie or something?" she asked him. "You already made your order."

"You trying to get rid of me?" he asked. He glanced behind him at the empty coffee shop. "It's not like I'm holding up the line."

"Maybe I have a hot date," she told him. She liked the way his brow tensed slightly. It was almost like he was jealous.

"A hot date at ten in the morning?" he asked.

She shrugged. "I can have a hot date whenever I want."

His green eyes narrowed. "He wouldn't happen to be about one foot tall, twenty pounds and has a love of drool?"

"I can't help the men I date," she replied. "And I happen to find short, chubby, mama's boys adorable. The kisses are out of this world."

Mr. Weathers laughed, making Emma's stomach tighten with lust. He had a great laugh. It was no wonder that women fell over themselves to sleep with him. He was smart, funny, good looking, and sexy as hell.

The fact that the women never stayed long said that he didn't like commitment. He was just in it for the fun. She could never date a man like that.

"I'm afraid I don't see the appeal," he said. "I like my dates a little older."

She chuckled. "Yeah, my baby dates aren't so good at fancy restaurants. Definite downside."

She grinned at him and he chuckled again.

"Have a great day, Emma," he said, casually strolling to the pickup window and taking his coffee. She loved that he knew her name. He came in every morning and they always had a fun, easy banter that left a smile on her face.

He dropped a twenty in her tip jar and sauntered out of the coffee shop and into the building lobby. She could watch that man walk anywhere. The way he moved was sexy and confident. It was no surprise to her that he was a billionaire CEO with the world at his feet.

"Emma, clean up the spill by the trash and you can go on break," her boss called to her.

She shook herself from watching Mr. Weathers walk away and picked up a cleaning towel. One day, she was going to get out of here. She had dreams and plans, and none of them revolved around cleaning up spilled coffee.

The mess by the trash can required a mop. She sighed and wondered just how she got here. Her dream job was never to be a barista. She had dreams of being something more, but her debt was out of control. She had a bachelor's degree, but no experience. No experience meant no career. No career meant no money, so she was stuck here selling coffee. She had to pay off those student loans somehow. No matter how hard she worked, it felt like she was barely treading water. Something needed to change.

Emma quickly mopped up, washed her hands, and went to go play with the baby.

Sam reached for her as soon as he saw her coming to their table. She loved the way his chubby little arms stretched out and the way his smile lit up. She wanted to be a mother, but with no boyfriend and no money, she didn't see it in the cards for a long time.

Yet one more thing life didn't seem to want to give her.

"Sammy," she cooed, pulling him in for a hug. She breathed in the sweet scent of baby shampoo, milk, and applesauce. He smelled like heaven.

"So, what are we going to do tonight?" she asked Sam.

He babbled something and gnawed on his cookie.

"Sounds like a plan to me," Emma agreed.

"I can't thank you enough for taking him," Grace said, sipping on her coffee. "I love this kid, but I need a break."

"I'm excited to watch him," Emma admitted. "I feel like all I do is work and pay off bills. Playing with him will be a welcome break."

She grinned and made faces at the baby. Sammy laughed like she was the funniest thing he'd ever seen. Emma giggled and snuggled him closer to her.

"You're going to make an awesome mom someday," Grace

said, watching her with a smile. "We just have to find you the right guy."

"I can't see it happening anytime soon," Emma warned her.

Grace shrugged. "I guess we can always dream. Sammy needs a buddy."

ackson

"What in the hell were you thinking?"

The sound of the newspaper hitting Jackson Weathers' desk was almost as loud as Jane's question. Jackson looked up from his work to see a very angry woman glaring at him.

"Just what in the hell were you thinking?" Jane repeated, her voice low and dangerous. She motioned to the newspaper. "Do you know how hard I have been working to change your image? And then you go and pull this shit?"

Jackson glanced down at the paper to see the headline: *"BILLIONAIRE PUBLIC SEX SCANDAL."* He had made front page news. Again.

"I don't remember doing that," he said, frowning and looking closer at the picture. The picture was censored, but it was clearly him balls deep in some blonde chick at a bar. "It's not really a flattering angle."

"You bastard," Jane whispered. She shook her head. Her normally neat bun was coming undone and gray wisps of hair framed her face. "I can't believe you'd do this."

"Do what?" Jackson scoffed. "The woman was of age and very consenting."

"You were in public," Jane hissed through gritted teeth.

"We weren't supposed to be, but that was half the fun," Jackson admitted. He looked a little closer at the picture again. "I think her name was Heidi?"

"It was *Tiffany*. And she also says that you then had her sister come and join you after you trashed the bar. With a bar fight. It's really thrilling reading."

"Oh, yes. I remember Brittany. Those two were tigers in the sack." Jackson smiled with the memory.

"Are you seriously not seeing the problem here?" Jane asked him, her hand going to her head like she had a headache.

"That I didn't get their numbers? Or perhaps that there was a photographer at a private party taking pictures without consent?"

"No." Jane narrowed her eyes at him. "It's that your business is going down the drain and the only way to save it is to clean up your reputation. You tell me that you'll keep your hands to yourself for a bit and stay out of trouble. And then you pour gasoline and light a match to destroy everything we've worked *months* for."

"This is not my fault. You said to keep a low profile. This was a private party. I don't even know how this photo got out."

Jane rubbed the bridge of her nose. "Getting into a fist fight is not low profile. Fucking a girl on the bar is not low profile. Having a threesome with her and her sister in the hot tub of the hotel is not keeping a low profile. It doesn't matter what the hell kind of party it was."

"At least they had a good time," Jackson replied with a smirk. He remembered now. It had been a great night. He leaned back in his office chair, keeping his cool.

"Right." Jane glared at him. "Telling them to get lost after was a nice touch. Very gentlemanly. It's really selling your product for you."

"This will blow over in a couple of days," Jackson told her. He sounded more confident than he felt. He'd never seen Jane this angry. The PR woman was usually the epitome of calm, always rolling with the punches. Physically, Jane reminded him of his very Italian grandmother, so her being angry was not a pleasant experience.

"It will not 'blow over.'" Jane sighed and smoothed her hair back into the neat bun at the back of her head. "Sales are already down. The stock price is already down. The comments on our social media ads are out of control."

"It can't be that bad. It's never that bad."

Jane pulled out her phone and cleared her throat. "I used to love W&W products for my baby, but now I won't buy them ever again. The owner is a horrible human being who obviously only cares about money and women. Why in the world would I buy diapers from him? Hash tag #lostcustomer and hash tag #FireWeathers."

Jackson shrugged. "There are always negative reviews."

"There are over three thousand like that on an ad that only ran for five hours," Jane informed him. "We had to stop running the ad because of the negative comments. Our moderators couldn't keep up with them. Hash tag #FireWeathers is trending right now."

Jackson felt a cold settle over his shoulders. This could be bad.

"So, we change advertisements. I lay low," Jackson replied.

Jane shook her head. "The board of directors is done with you. They're starting to talk about kicking you out."

"They can't do that," Jackson said, anger heating his voice just slightly. "This is my company. This is my father's company."

"They can if you are a detriment to profits." Jane motioned to the newspaper. "Which you are. Your playboy antics are hurting your company and given the evidence, you don't care. That story isn't the first one to blow up since you were supposed to lay low."

"The board shouldn't care about this kind of thing," Jackson said. The newspaper no longer felt silly. It felt like it might turn into a snake and bite him.

"And if your antics weren't costing them money, they wouldn't. You can't treat women like that and not expect a backlash."

"They consent," Jackson informed her. "They come up to me and ask for this. They want their fifteen minutes of fame and are willing to use their bodies to get it. I'm not going to say no to a good time."

Jane sighed. "I know you aren't a bad guy." She looked over at the newspaper. "But no one else does. They just see the headlines. And the headlines aren't good."

"What do you know about the board?" Jackson asked, pointedly looking away from the paper. "How much time?"

"Not long. This latest advertising blowup has them all riled. They want you gone," Jane told him. "And right now, they're right. You are costing profits."

"I'm not losing my company," Jackson growled. He got up and paced behind his desk. "What do I do?"

"Other than resign with what I assume you consider dignity?"

Jackson gave her an annoyed look. "Yes."

She evaluated him for a moment, her dark eyes looking him over. Once again, he was reminded of the way his grandmother used to look at him. The only difference was that Grandmother liked to hold a wooden spoon as a threat.

"I have a nuclear option," she told him. "You aren't going to like it. It's something the board can't know you planned, but if you do it, they will leave you alone. It will let you keep your company."

Jackson sat down behind his desk. "Tell me."

"You need a wife and a baby," Jane told him.

Jackson couldn't help but let out a quick laugh. "How in the world is a wife and a baby going to save my company?" he asked, leaning back in his big office chair. His kept his expression easy, despite the difficult nature of the discussion. He always appeared calm. It was how he successfully ran a business.

"You need to change your image," Jane told him. The slender woman settled into the over-sized leather seat facing the desk and got comfortable. She crossed her legs at the ankle and once again smoothed her graying hair back into her bun.

"Isn't that what you were supposed to be doing?" Jackson asked.

"It was, until you made headline news negating everything I've done," Jane replied coolly. "There is no amount of photoshoots of you holding babies that can fix this."

"I thought you said the baby ads were working," Jackson countered. "That they upped sales."

"They helped, but your competition is a loving mother and her two adorable kids," Jane said. "She's beating you in every demographic because she's real. Your customers relate to her. They don't relate to you."

"But her prices are twice what mine are," Jackson countered. "People prefer cheap."

"True," Jane acknowledged, bowing her head slightly. "However, her numbers are going up and yours are going down. Cheap isn't winning anymore. You need people to want to buy what you represent. You need people to trust you. "

"What's not to trust?" Jackson asked, giving Jane a winning smile. His blue eyes sparkled.

"That." She pointed to his grin and then his whole body. "You exude confidence and charm. You're full of easy sex appeal."

"And what's wrong with that?" He asked her, still giving her the full Jackson Weathers' smile. It had the effect of making women drop their panties and willingly give themselves to him on a regular basis.

"You want to know what's wrong with that?" Jane didn't seem affected by his smile. If anything, she seemed annoyed. "You sell diapers. No one wants to buy sexy diapers."

Jackson let the megawatt smile fade. It wasn't working on her anyway.

"You are known as a playboy. You have a different model or actress in your bed every other night. And that was fine until the Innocence Company started cashing in on the sweet nature of Jessica Balboa. She's a mother that other mothers want to emulate."

"And that's not me," Jackson agreed.

Jane stood up from the chair and put her hands on the front of the desk.

"You hired me, Mr. Weathers, to fix the fact that every single one of your products is down this year," Jane told him. She was all confidence. "Your brand hasn't changed. Your prices and suppliers are all the same. The only difference now is the competition. And that means that we have to beat the Innocence Company at their own game if you want to be king again. You need to be the face that mothers want to trust their babies with. Right now, I wouldn't trust you with a houseplant."

Jackson evaluated Jane for a moment before speaking. He hated that she was making sense. The only change in the market was the addition of a new player. Jessica Balboa's Innocence Company was doing something he wasn't.

"So, you want me to get married and have a baby," he repeated back. "What if that's not what I want? I'm not exactly looking to change my ways. I rather like a different model or actress in my bed every other night."

"And I'm not telling you that you can't," Jane replied, standing up straight. "Once you have this set up and people trust you again, you can go back to being the bad-boy billionaire. Until then, you have to be the epitome of fatherly love and trust. And that means no screwing up. I don't care if it's in a private setting or not. This is all or nothing. You can't accidentally slip up with this."

She pointedly looked at the newspaper. He would have to say goodbye to his fun for a while if he agreed to this. He could understand that. If he had a wife and child, there was no way he could even go to a party where women threw themselves at him.

It would be a difficult change. He wasn't just reducing the sex he had with random beautiful women. He'd be giving it up.

"And if I don't do this? If I hire someone else to fix the brand?"

Jane shrugged. "Your sales are down twenty percent this year and dropping. Last year, it was ten. Since the article ran, we've had two stores refuse to carry you. You can do the math on how long you have before the board kicks you out."

She was right. Something had to change. As much as he hated it, the change was going to have to be from him.

Jackson sighed. "And you're sure? You're sure that this is the only way to salvage this?"

"We've done countless market surveys. Mothers don't

trust you, and thus don't trust your brand. If you sold condoms, you'd be a billionaire."

"I *am* a billionaire," Jackson corrected her.

Jane shrugged. "For how long? You can't keep losing sales to the Innocence Company."

Jackson stood from his desk and stared out the window at the city skyline. It was early summer, which meant that all the women were out in flowery dresses and starting to show skin with the warmer weather. His favorite time of year.

His eyes looked over to the photo on his desk. The black and white photo held a seven-year-old little boy pretending to answer the phone while his father smiled at him from the background. Jackson remembered that day in his father's office. It was the day that Jackson knew his future was with this company. His future was W&W BabyCo.

W&W had started out as a part-time idea from his father. With his father's hard work, the company had grown, but it was Jackson who'd made it into a billion dollar enterprise. He'd taken his father's small diaper company and created a line of baby care items the world couldn't live without.

Until now.

He was watching his success, and with it his father's memory, slowly fade. Something had to change.

"You're sure?" Jackson turned from the frame and looked out the window at the city below.

"Positive," Jane assured him. "In every test group, showing you as a caring father made people trust your brand again."

He turned slowly. "And it'll all be for show?"

Jane shrugged. "If that's what you want. It has to be believable, though. Mothers have to believe that you've left your wanton ways and settled down."

"That might be harder than it sounds," Jackson replied. He rather liked his wanton ways. They were a part of who he was. How could he possibly be with only one woman? It sounded like torture.

But losing his company was a worse torture.

"It's only for a couple years," Jane reminded him. "Once the public trusts you again, you can go back to your old ways. Albeit, you'll have to be a little more discreet. As long as the public thinks of you as a caring father, your sales will reflect that."

Jackson sighed. This wasn't going to be an easy thing to do. He liked his life. He liked knowing that he could have any woman he wanted. His world revolved around women and his company. He was going to have to give one of them up.

"And the children?" Jackson asked, raising an eyebrow at Jane. "You're sure just getting a wife won't do it? I need a kid?"

"You sell diapers, not women's items. People need to believe that you would use these products yourself, not that you're just hawking them like a used car salesman. They need to believe you."

"So the kid is non-negotiable?" He didn't like the idea of bringing a baby into this world just to make him some money. It felt cheap and underhanded.

"Yes," Jane replied with a nod. "It's the key selling point. You need a kid."

The more he considered the idea of the public trusting him with a baby, the more it made sense. He knew that his actions were hurting the company. He needed to change what the public thought of him. He needed to look like someone who would have a reason to sell diapers and baby supplies. He needed to be a trusted source, not just a supplier.

He also knew that if he was going to bring a child into the world, he was going to be a father to it. The mother could come and go, but the baby would most certainly be his. He would make sure that kid had everything it could ever want.

He looked at the photo again and thought of his own father. The man had been stern but kind. Jackson rather liked the idea of raising a son like his father had raised him. It was something he could get behind. He'd never really envisioned himself a father, but that didn't mean he couldn't be an amazing one.

Just because he wasn't good at sticking with women didn't mean he couldn't be good at sticking with kids. Kids were special.

"How will we convince my new wife?" he asked Jane. "Marrying me is easy money, but having a baby? That's a little more complicated."

"It's not like you have a hard time convincing women to sleep with you," Jane replied with a shrug. "It's not a big step from there."

She had a point. It was rather ironic, actually. For the past few years, he'd been doing everything he could to prevent having a child. He'd gone out of his way to make sure he didn't knock up one of his one-night stands looking for an easy meal-ticket in the shape of child support. Now, he was going to have to try for that exact outcome.

He looked at the picture of him and his father again. Jackson could do this. He could find someone that would play the part. And he would love the child. Staying away from women wouldn't be the end of the world. And if it would save his business, he would do anything.

Time held for a moment, the way it always did right before he made a big decision.

"Okay." He hated the way his stomach twisted. "I'll do it. For the company."

"Excellent, sir," Jane said with a hard smile. "I have a list of potential brides for you. They're all in advertising, so they know what to do. I can have the agreement and a pre-nup to you by the end of the day."

Jackson nodded, feeling like he was being led by the nose to slaughter. This was how stallions felt on their way to become geldings.

"I would recommend choosing someone that you get along well with, so I'll have you do some interviews first. You need someone bright and bubbly. You should like her and most importantly, the public should like her. She needs to be good with kids, especially babies."

The phrase, "bright and bubbly" stuck out in Jackson's mind. *Good with kids.* He looked away from his desk and directly at Jane.

"You want someone to rival Jessica?" A thought was already turning in his head. "Someone who is sweet and kind, loves kids, and would look good on a billboard?"

Jane nodded. "Not model good. Mother good. She needs to be attractive, but more girl-next-door and less your usual Barbie-doll. The market must believe that she's a real person."

Jackson smiled. He already knew the perfect woman for the job. Someone he got along with and was possibly the most cheerful person he'd ever met.

"I won't need your candidates," Jackson informed Jane. "I have someone in mind. As long as I can convince her, she'll be perfect."

Jane looked at him. "Just give her that smile you gave me earlier and she'll say yes to anything you ask. I would have married you on the spot if you'd asked me, and I'm already married."

Jackson grinned. He thought he'd lost his touch with Jane, but he still had it. He really could get to any woman in the world with that smile.

CHAPTER 3

 ackson

Jackson's hands sweated. They were sticky and hot, and he wiped them nervously on his pants the entire way down the elevator.

He hadn't been this nervous since junior high.

Asking out women was easy. He could smile and get any woman he wanted to hop in his bed for the night with hardly any effort. However, the idea of asking Emma to marry him and have his child to save his company made him nervous.

So, halfway down to the lobby, he decided he wasn't going to ask her directly. He was going to take her to dinner. That made his palms dry a little, but his heart still raced in his chest. She still made him nervous. She had turned him down before. She was one of the few women that consistently told him no.

He didn't know why she said no to him. As far as he

knew, she wasn't seeing anyone, and even if she was, he was fucking Jackson Weathers. No woman said no to him. The fact that she could say no actually made him like her more. She was unobtainable.

Maybe that was why his hands shook as the elevator doors opened. Maybe that was why the butterflies in his stomach suddenly came to life. He had done hundreds of high power meetings with men and women worth billions, their entire companies on the line, and he hadn't been this nervous.

It had to be her. Emma was special.

He took a deep breath, licked his lips, put on his smile, and walked into the coffee shop.

She was at the register counting change out for a customer. He watched her for a moment. Her dark hair was pulled back in a simple ponytail under her company hat. He'd never seen it down, yet he had a feeling it would look lovely framing her slender face and big hazel eyes.

She wasn't model skinny, which he actually liked. She had real curves to her body that his hands ached to hold onto. She was real, which after dating hundreds of fake women, was suddenly very appealing. His hands started to shake again.

"Mr. Weathers, you're back." She looked up at him and her smile lit up her face. He felt warm just being with her and those damn butterflies kicked it up a notch.

"Hello, Emma," he greeted her. His voice cracked.

"What can I get you?" she asked, ignoring his voice crack for which he was thankful. How did she make him feel like a sixteen-year-old boy just by smiling at him?

"Actually, I'd like to get you something," he told her. He leaned casually against the counter. "I'd like to get you dinner tonight."

"Tonight?" Her eyes went wide.

"If you're available." His stomach knotted waiting for her to answer.

She chewed her bottom lip for a moment. "I can't."

"You already have a date?" he asked. He hated that his chest tightened. Damn the man that was taking his spot.

"Kind of," she replied. She gave him a crooked smile. "He's one. Remember how I said I like bald, chubby, toothless guys?"

It took him a moment to understand what she was saying.

"I'm babysitting tonight," she clarified. She blushed, putting color in her cheeks that made him wonder where else she flushed when she was nervous. "But, I'm free tomorrow."

Hope surged in his chest and he let out a breath he didn't know he was holding. He'd asked her out before this, so he wasn't sure why he was struggling with this now. Asking women out was kind of his specialty.

"Tomorrow is great," he told her. He grinned. "I'll pick you up at seven."

She winced. "Can you do eight? I work until seven."

Not a lot of women had the gall to change the time of a date with a billionaire, and they both knew it. She wasn't making this easy. However, he smiled. "Eight it is. I'll pick you up here."

"Sure." She looked like she wanted to say more.

"What?"

"What should I wear?" She gave a nervous laugh. "I think the nicest dress I own is acceptable for Olive Garden, and I don't see you taking me to Olive Garden."

"Do you want to go to Olive Garden?" he asked her. He liked that she was blushing again.

"We can," she told him. "It just doesn't seem your style. You seem... fancier."

He grinned. "I am fancier," he assured her. "How about I

take care of everything? You just finish your shift, and I'll take care of everything else."

She frowned. "What should I wear, though?"

"I'll take care of that," he told her. She didn't look convinced. "I'll get you something. And before you say I shouldn't, I will remind you that I am a billionaire. And kind of your boss."

"You are not my boss," she replied, shaking her head.

"I own the building," he said.

"Yes, but you don't own Coffee Shack. I work for Coffee Shack. You can't fire me. You can kick my employer out of the building, but you can't directly fire me. So, you're not my boss," she explained. He liked the way she smiled as she said it.

"Well, that's good then," he smiled. "I don't have to worry about any of those pesky employee dating rules."

She giggled and it made his chest tighten. How in the world was he still nervous? She already said yes to the date.

"Can I ask you something?" He kept leaning on the counter, trying to keep playing it cool. "I've asked you out before. Why did you say yes this time?"

She shrugged. "Because this time you meant it."

Her answer threw him off guard. Where normally he would have been able to hold a smile, he was unable to this time. "I meant it every time."

She shook her head slightly. "Not like this. This time you're actually asking me. It's different somehow this time. You mean it."

She had no idea how right she was. "I'm glad you said yes," he told her.

She grinned. "Me too."

"So, I'll pick you up here tomorrow at eight. Be ready for the time of your life," he told her. He was already thinking of the best way to get her to like him. He was going to show her a great time so she'd want to say yes to his proposal to marry him and have his baby.

"Okay." She grinned and hugged her arms to her body. "That sounds great."

He flashed her his best smile and walked out of the coffee shop feeling like he'd just won the lottery. She had said yes. He felt like jumping into the air and shouting, but decided to just walk calmly to the elevator since he knew she was watching.

He grinned the whole way up. This was going to work.

mma

The clock read 6:58. She only had two minutes left of work and then she had no idea what was going to happen next. She was supposed to go on a date with billionaire Jackson Weathers in an hour, but she had no idea where they were going, what they were doing, or what she was supposed to wear.

She'd packed a small backpack with a cute little black dress, but she wasn't sure it was going to work if he wanted to take her somewhere nice. She looked down at her khaki pants to see a new coffee stain. There was no way she could wear her work outfit anywhere.

"Excuse me, are you Miss Emma Sheridan?"

A man in a dark brown suit stood at the front of the coffee shop. Everything about him was thin and nervous looking from his brown suit to his wispy brown hair.

"That's me," Emma told him, coming out from behind the counter. The clock tripped over to seven.

"My name is Thad Romero," the man told her. He smoothed the top of his thinning hair. "I'm here to help you dress."

Emma blinked twice. No one had helped dress her since she was five years old and couldn't get the buttons straight on her sweaters. "Excuse me?"

"Mr. Weathers has instructed me to help you pick out something appropriate for this evening," the man explained. "If you'll come with me, we can begin."

Emma stood still for a moment before remembering that Mr. Weathers had said he would take care of everything. She wasn't sure what she'd been expecting, but this certainly wasn't it. With a shrug, she followed this thin man out into the main building.

He walked quickly and efficiently to the elevator, holding the door open for her and then pressing the button to the thirty-third floor. As the doors closed and the elevator began moving, he put his hands on Emma's shoulders and moved her to the center of the elevator.

"The light is not ideal in here, but we are pressed for time," he told her as he circled around her, examining her like a hungry shark. He reached up and took her chin in his hand, studying her face. "Hazel eyes? The greens then."

Emma just stared at him, unsure of what she'd gotten herself into. When the elevator door opened, the man hurried out into the hallway and was halfway to a door when he turned around.

"Well? Hurry up, we don't have much time," the man said, holding open a door and motioning impatiently.

Emma shook herself and quickly followed him. The door looked like it should lead to a conference room, but instead of an over-sized table and chairs, there were racks of clothing. She glanced around and saw two women waiting at a full makeup counter, complete with the movie-set lights.

"This is Claire and Shana," Thad explained, pushing her into the room. "They're here to do your hair and makeup once I've fitted you. Come stand here, please."

Thad had her stand on a small stool. He pulled out a tape measure and quickly measured her hips, waist and bust with speed and accuracy. He kept muttering the numbers and looking around as he thought.

Suddenly, he paused and smiled. "It's perfect."

"What's perfect?" Emma asked, but he didn't answer her.

Instead, he dove into a rack of clothing and sorted through it until coming to a specific hanger. He pulled it out and smiled at her.

"I'll have this ready in just a few moments," he told her. "If you'll please go to Claire, she'll get you started. Claire? Half up-do, please."

The taller woman in the corner stepped forward and smiled. "Please sit. I'm going to do your hair. Shana will do your makeup. Do you have any allergies or specific requests?"

"Um, no allergies," Emma replied. "I guess my only request is a more natural look."

"Oh, with your skin, that will be perfect," Shana told her. "You're going to look like a million dollars."

"Okay." Emma wasn't sure what exactly was going on, but she was willing to go with it. Apparently, she was getting a dress, hair, and makeup to go out with Mr. Weathers. When he said he would take care of things, he meant it.

Shana and Claire talked between themselves as they worked. It was the same comforting talk Emma had heard in every beauty parlor and hair salon her whole life and she found it soothing. It was all gossip and interesting tidbits of other people's lives.

"I probably shouldn't say this, given that he's paying us, but did you see the website?" Shana asked. Emma looked up at her curious.

"What website?" she asked.

"It's called the 'Bedpost' and people can make notches on celebrities' bedposts. You know, if you sleep with them," Shana explained. "A lot of them are unsubstantiated, but you should see Jackson Weathers. It's a lot."

"Yeah?" Emma felt her stomach twist a little. She didn't like thinking of Mr. Weathers like that.

"You know what, don't look it up until after your date, sweetie," Claire advised. "Have fun with him, but be warned. The man is a heart-breaker."

"What makes you say that?" Emma asked. Claire clicked her curling iron into place in Emma's dark hair.

"This isn't the first time we've done this for him," Claire told her. "We don't do it often, so you should definitely feel special. But, you're not the first and you won't be the last."

"This is something he only does for girls he really trying to impress," Shana added.

"Oh?" Emma's stomach twisted a little more.

Shana nodded. "My advice? Enjoy every minute. The guy is loaded and he knows how to spend. Just don't expect him to call you tomorrow."

"Oh, I didn't," Emma assured the two women.

"You're sweet," Claire told her. "We're only telling you this so you don't get your heart broken. He's not a long-term kind of guy."

Emma nodded. "I kind of figured that. He seems like a love 'em and leave 'em kind of guy."

"Very," Shana assured her. She pulled back and smiled. "Perfect. What do you think?"

Shana held up a small handheld mirror for Emma to inspect her makeup work. Emma gasped. She looked like a movie star. Her eyes were bigger and brighter, her skin flawless and somehow, Shana had even gotten her nose to look a little smaller.

"Shana's the best," Claire agreed. "I'll be done in two minutes, Thad."

"Good," Thad said, coming up behind them. "We only have five minutes to finish."

Claire finished pinning the curls to Emma's head, humming and fixing as she went until she smiled. "Perfect."

With that, Thad hustled Emma over and into a changing area. He handed her a dress made of green satin.

"Take everything off. And I do mean everything. Underwear will show under this dress." He motioned her into the changing area without letting her say a word in protest. "Step into the dress, please. Not over-head or you'll mess up your hair."

Emma looked around at the curtains for a second before stripping down. She folded her clothes into a neat pile on the floor next to her, feeling exposed as she stepped into the dress. The satin was cold against her skin as she shimmied it up her legs and over her chest. She slid her arms into the delicate shoulders straps and pulled the dress up.

Thad pulled back the curtain and zipped her up before she had a chance to even call him. The zipper went up like butter, but it fit her every curve.

"Good," Thad said, checking her form. "Some simple shoes and you'll be ready. And right on time, too."

He pulled her out into the main room again and handed her a pair of green strappy heels that matched the dress. Bowing before her, he helped her put them on.

It was then that she saw herself in the mirror and gasped.

The dress was amazing. The hair was amazing. The makeup was amazing. She looked like a princess in a fairy tale about to meet her Prince Charming at the ball. The emerald green of the dress brought out the green in her eyes and the darkness of her hair. Soft curls of her hair fell like perfect paint strokes to complement everything.

She didn't know that she could look this beautiful.

"You clean up nicely," Shana told her, smiling at her from across the room.

"We're late," Thad announced, taking her hand and pulling her to the door. "Mr. Weathers is expecting you now."

With that he hurried her out of the room as she shouted thanks to Claire and Shana. It was on the ride down the elevator that her stomach started to unravel. She was nervous now. She had been fine until she thought about Mr. Weathers seeing her like this.

He'd only ever seen her with her hair up in a ponytail and hidden under a hat. She'd never worn a dress around him, let alone a ball gown. Khaki pants, black polo shirt, and a green apron were the only thing he'd ever seen her in.

The idea of suddenly being beautiful in front of the man she loved to flirt with was suddenly very daunting. When the elevator doors opened, she couldn't move. She was frozen.

"Come on," Thad said gently, taking her hand and pulling her into the empty lobby.

Her heels clicked on the marble floors as she held up the hem of her dress and walked to the coffee shop. It felt ridiculous to be this dressed up and going to the shop, but since that was where he was meeting her, that's where she went.

With only a few steps left to go, Thad jumped out in front of her and made sure everything was perfect. He smoothed a flyaway hair from her face and adjusted the collar on her dress to lay flat.

"You look like a princess," he told her with a thin smile. "Have fun and don't worry about the dress. Mr. Weathers already paid for it. Same with the shoes."

He did one final check before moving out of the way and letting her finish walking to the coffee shop.

Emma swallowed hard. She knew she didn't have a reason to be nervous, but the butterflies were still mamboing around in her stomach like there was no tomorrow. She'd had hundreds of conversations with Mr. Weathers. She knew that she would have a wonderful time tonight, and yet for some reason her heart was pounding and her mouth suddenly went dry.

"Wow," she heard a voice say behind her...

mma

She spun to see Mr. Weathers leaning against the window to the coffee shop entrance. He wore a jet black suit that fit his broad shoulders and lean waist. He looked like he belonged on the cover of GQ. His perfect blond hair was somehow more perfect as he walked over.

"Hi." She wished she had something clever to say, but the only thing she could think of was *"Welcome to the Coffee Shack,"* and somehow that didn't feel appropriate.

"You look absolutely stunning," he told her. "I'm going to have the prettiest date at the restaurant."

She grinned, enjoying the compliment. "Thank you." She smoothed the green satin of her dress. "This is amazing and so much more than anything I could have expected."

He grinned. "That's kind of the point."

Her smile widened. No wonder women fell over themselves to be with him. "Well, thank you."

"Let me see you spin," he requested.

She slowly spun in a circle, loving the way the heavy fabric took the motion and swirled around her ankles when she finished.

"Beautiful," he said, his green eyes sparkling. She believed him. Even though he was the world's biggest flirt, she believed that he found her beautiful. "Are you ready to eat?"

"Starving," she admitted. "I didn't get much of a break today."

"Then right this way." He led her out to the front entrance. A cherry red sports car sat idling on the curb.

"That's yours?" she asked, pointing to the car.

"Unless you know someone else who drives one of these," he replied, going to the passenger door and holding it open for her. "There's only six in the world."

"Oh. I think there's several million of my car," she replied. "So, nearly the same thing."

He chuckled and she caught the scent of his cologne as she settled in the car. He smelled of clean springs and slightly of mint. He carefully closed the door behind her, making sure her skirt didn't catch, and ran around to the driver's side.

Once he sat down, he turned and looked over at her. "You ready?"

He revved the engine and she giggled. The whole car shook with power. Without waiting for her answer, he peeled out into the street, letting the sports car zoom and speed away. The car reacted to his slightest touch, turning and speeding as he drove through the city. She didn't know where they were going, and honestly she didn't care.

She was in a fancy dress in a fancy car on her way to a fancy restaurant with a handsome and charming man. She was half afraid that if she closed her eyes, she'd open them to find this was all just a wonderful and crazy dream.

"Here we are," he said, pulling into a parking lot. The restaurant's green sign lit up the night.

Olive Garden.

She started to laugh. "Now I'm overdressed," she told him. "It is my idea of fancy, though."

He grinned and gunned the engine again, pulling back out onto the main road. In just a few more moments, they were in the ritzier part of town.

Emma didn't come to this area very often. She didn't have the funds to spend thousands of dollars on a purse or to eat hundred dollar meals. It was fun to walk around and look at the lavish things for sale, but she didn't do it often. It was too far outside her price range to even look.

"Here we are," he repeated, pulling into the valet station. The building looked more like a Tuscan mansion than a restaurant.

"So am I to understand that there will be no Olive Garden?" she asked, making him smile.

The valet opened the door to the red sports car and she carefully stepped out. Moving in the long skirt took planning so she didn't trip over the soft satin fabric.

Mr. Weathers was right at her arm, guiding her into the restaurant. It felt like something out of a movie. This was how kings and queens walked into buildings.

The feeling didn't stop there. At the reception desk, the staff immediately jumped to attention as they walked in. They didn't have to give their names or stop to get a table. A man that Emma assumed was the manager escorted them directly to a table next to the window with the best view of the sunset in the state. Mr. Weathers held out her chair for her to sit.

"Champagne?" Mr. Weathers asked, pointing to a bottle cooling next to their table. It looked like one of the fancy brands they kept behind the counter at the liquor store.

"Sure," Emma replied, settling into her seat. She picked up a menu as Mr. Weathers poured her a glass. The prices alone made her eyes bug out. There was no inexpensive option. She swallowed hard.

"Cheers," Mr. Weathers said, holding out her glass. She tapped her glass against his and took a sip. The tiny bubbles tickled her nose. "And don't look at the menu. The chef is making something special for us."

"Oh." She set the menu down. "This is amazing, by the way."

"Well, I am trying to impress you."

Emma grinned. "I think it might be working."

He flashed that grin that made her knees go weak, and suddenly she remembered she wasn't wearing any panties. Her legs rubbed together and she tried to take a sip of champagne to distract herself.

"So, tell me Mr. Weathers, what do you like to do for fun?" she asked him.

"Please, call me Jackson." He took a sip of champagne. "I like to race cars, I like to travel, and I enjoy trying new things."

The way his eyes sparkled made her think that each one of those things had something to do with sex. She pressed her legs together a little harder.

"What do you like to do?" he asked, his voice smooth like silk. He watched her with those green eyes of his, following her like she was something amazing.

"Um, I like to babysit for my friend," she replied, feeling like that wasn't nearly as good an answer as driving fast cars. "I also like to paint. And swim."

"What kind of painting?" he asked, looking genuinely interested.

"Watercolors, mostly. I'm not very good yet, but it's fun."

"I would imagine you are better than you let on," he said,

sipping at his champagne again. She felt her cheeks heat at the compliment.

"Excuse me, sir," a waiter interrupted the silence as she flushed. "Your first course."

The waiter set down two plates in front of them and Emma's mouth started to water. The plate itself was artwork, with three mushrooms painted with creamy melted cheese.

"Bacon and cream cheese mushrooms," Jackson told her, picking up his fork. "They're my favorite appetizer."

"I can see why," she said, taking a small bite. Delicious flavor washed over her tongue. They were the best mushrooms she'd ever eaten. "So good."

He grinned and took a bite off his own plate. "I'm glad you like them. Means we have similar tastes."

She quickly swallowed a bigger bite. "I think anyone would like these. They're amazing."

He chuckled. "You'd be surprised how many women have told me they won't eat these. Either it's the bacon, the cream cheese, or that they're on a juice diet. I've had many tell me that these aren't their cup of tea."

"Why would you come to a restaurant like this if you were on a juice diet?" Emma asked, quickly finishing off her last mushroom. She wished she had more because she was hungry and those were delicious. She felt like she could eat an entire dozen and still want more.

"I have no idea, actually," Jackson replied with a laugh. "So, tell me, why do you work at the Coffee Shack?"

Emma smiled, but it was more reflex than joy. "It's a job. It pays the bills."

"So your dream isn't to be a barista?" Jackson asked.

She shook her head. "No. I want to be a marine biologist, but so far I haven't really gotten the opportunity."

"What's stopping you?"

She sighed and played with her fork on the empty plate.

"What's stopping you, Emma?" he repeated, this time more gently.

"Bills." She hated that she felt embarrassed.

"Bills?"

"School loans and medical debt. I went to an expensive undergrad and got a degree in biology," she explained. "Then I had a pretty major car accident that created a lot of medical bills right after I graduated."

"I see," he said, finishing the last bite of his own mushroom. There was no judgment in his voice, just understanding.

"So, that's why I work at Coffee Shack. Until I get those debts paid off, I will do just about any job that pays me." She shrugged and tried to smile. "Someday, I plan on going back to school so I can get my dream job. I just have to pay some things off first."

Jackson leaned back with a smooth motion. "It sounds like you have a plan."

"I just have something that looks like a plan," she admitted. She fiddled with her napkin and tried to think of a way to change the conversation. She was sure she was making a great impression on her billionaire date telling him all about how she was broke.

"The second course," the waiter announced, taking advantage of the brief lull between the two of them to place fresh plates and a full bowl of something amazing in front of Emma. She'd never had such service.

"Lobster bisque," Jackson informed her as she picked up her spoon.

"I love lobster. How is it that you're picking all my favorites?"

He grinned. "Luck. They're my favorites, too."

She smiled and took a sip of the soup. It was heaven in a

spoonful. The bisque was hearty while the lobster had sweetness.

"You like it?" Jackson asked, watching her reaction.

"I love it. I think I could eat this every day and never get tired of it."

He grinned, enjoying her reaction.

"So, tell me about you," she said, pausing to enjoy her soup. "What's something that no one knows about Jackson Weathers."

"If I tell you, then someone will know," he replied. He took a sip of soup and sat thoughtfully for a moment. "I hate spiders. I can't stand them. Even the tiny ones."

"They're not so bad. They're very important to the ecosystem."

"Well, they're not important to the ecosystem of my office," he replied, making her laugh. She grinned.

This date was going better than she'd expected. The food was amazing, which she had been expecting, but the easy conversations they shared every morning while he ordered his coffee shone through. It was like getting an extra long version of the morning and she was enjoying it.

The next course was sea bass with truffle sauce, followed by a Cornish game hen with an amazing demi-glace that made her want to cry tears of joy. She'd never eaten anything as wonderful as this meal. Jackson kept her champagne glass filled and the conversation flowing.

Before she realized it, they'd been on their date for over two hours. She'd learned that he had no siblings and that both of his parents had died. It was just another thing that the two of them had in common. She felt such a connection to him, and it wasn't just the champagne.

She loved the way he looked at her like she mattered. She was someone to him, even if before today she was just the coffee girl. Even then, he'd known her name. He'd really know her name after tonight.

I'm going to sleep with him, she decided as they waited for the dessert course to arrive. She smiled at the thought. She knew that was probably his intention all along given his reputation, but she was enjoying her evening so much she was okay with it. It was going to be her choice.

"And for dessert, a chocolate fondue," he announced as the waiters set up the table with a chocolate stand and various plates full of dipping items. Strawberries, bananas, raspberries, cookies, marshmallows, and anything else that could be dipped in chocolate filled the table. There was no way she was going to be able to eat even half of it, but she was willing to give it a try.

"My favorite is the strawberries," he advised, showing her his dipping technique. He opened his mouth and carefully sucked the luscious red fruit into his mouth.

Emma swallowed hard and pressed her knees together.

Yup. Definitely sleeping with him.

"Here, have one," he offered, dipping a red berry into the dark chocolate and then holding it out for her. She leaned forward, her lips coming to wrap around the strawberry and brushing against his fingertips.

It was electric to touch him. He smiled.

"You have some chocolate on your cheek," he pointed out.

"Oh." She went to wipe her cheek, but he beat her to it. His hand caressed her skin and she shivered with pleasure.

He leaned forward, his hand on her cheek, and tipped his mouth to meet hers in a kiss.

He tasted like chocolate and wine and everything delicious in the world. His kiss was sweeter than any dessert and better than anything she could have imagined.

He kissed like he looked. Amazing.

She was definitely sleeping with him tonight. She'd never been this turned on with just a kiss.

He pulled back and smiled at her. She was all electric shivers and desire now.

"Can I ask you something?" Emma picked out a marshmallow and carefully dipped it in the chocolate.

"Anything," he replied. His green eyes sparkled in the candlelight of the restaurant.

"Why me?" she asked. "I mean, you can have any woman in the city. Why me?"

He swallowed and patted his mouth with a napkin. "I actually have an offer for you," he told her. "I wanted to take you on this date to see if we would be a good match, and I think we would."

"A good match?" She frowned, confused. "What could a coffee barista do for you?"

He smiled slowly. "For that, we'll need to go back to my place."

CHAPTER 6

 *mma*

Emma tried to keep her knee still. She tried not to bounce it up and down, but she couldn't help but move it. She was nervous now as the car sped along the road to Jackson Weathers' apartment and her knee couldn't hold it in.

Jackson had something planned for her. He wanted to discuss something, and she had no idea what it could possibly be. Plus, they were going to his house. Where he took all the women he slept with. Now that it was really happening, she was nervous.

She wasn't sure what was going to happen next.

He kept up comfortable small talk the entire short trip back to his luxury high rise apartment. If she hadn't been too busy thinking about the fact that she wasn't wearing panties, she would have been able to admire the building. It was old and beautiful with a literal golden elevator to bring them to the penthouse suite.

He scanned his thumbprint in the elevator and smiled at her.

"You're nervous, aren't you?" he asked.

"Maybe a little," she said. "I've never been in an elevator that requires a fingerprint."

He leaned over, his lips brushing the small hairs by her ear and making her body tingle. The movement was intimate. "And the fact that you aren't wearing underwear has nothing to do with it, right?"

She froze as he chuckled and pulled away. She did her best to stand up taller and compose herself.

"First, that's none of your business," she told him.

"And second?" he leaned against the elevator wall as they went up.

"I don't actually have a second," she admitted, making him chuckle.

The elevator came to a stop and the doors opened to reveal a regular looking door. Jackson walked over and placed his hand flat on the wood, just above the doorknob. The imprint of his hand started to glow and she heard the unmistakable sound of a lock opening. That was some high-tech door.

"Please, come in, Emma." He held open the door for her to step inside his home.

The high-rise apartment was bigger than her childhood home. Everything was modern with clean lines and crisp colors. It suited the image she had of Jackson in her mind. She could imagine him at home here.

He tossed his suit jacket on the back of a white leather couch and went to the kitchen table. Even though it was night, she could tell that his view from up here was absolutely amazing. She rather hoped she get a chance to see it in the morning.

Depending on what he had to tell her.

"I'll need you to sign this," he said, handing her a stack of legal papers. "It's a fairly standard non-disclosure agreement."

"Why do I need to sign an NDA?" She asked, tentatively taking the stack of paper.

"I have a proposal for you," he told her, sitting down at the table. "Sign that, and I'll tell you all about it."

Emma chewed on her bottom lip for a moment before taking a seat at the table. She quickly scanned the legal document, but it appeared to be the standard legalese mumbo jumbo of all legal documents. She could in no way talk to anyone about their conversation and if she did, she would have to pay so much money she would need to move to a third world country just to afford food.

Jackson slid a pen across the table and she carefully signed her name on the line.

"Do you do this with all your dates?" she teased, handing him the signed papers.

"Only the ones that I am going to ask to marry me," he replied.

Emma's heart did a full stop.

"Excuse me, what?"

"I need to find a wife," he replied. He was calm and collected like this was a normal discussion. Who knew? Maybe in his world it was.

"Most people just date," Emma replied. "There's a whole dating industry for just that reason."

Jackson smiled at her. "I need a wife and a child for business reasons. I'd like it to be you."

"Me?" She thought they had a connection, but to marry her? "I don't understand."

He stood up from the table and went to the kitchen. "Wine?" he asked, pulling out two glasses and then going to a fridge and pulling out an opaque bottle.

"Yes, please," she replied. Wine was definitely needed for this conversation.

"My business is struggling," he told her, uncorking the wine with practiced ease. "I have to update my image."

"Your image?"

"I'm a playboy. A womanizer," he said. He smiled at her. "You even remarked upon it."

"True," Emma agreed, thinking of the bedpost website. "But what does that have to do with your business?"

"Customers don't trust a womanizer to sell them diapers," he replied. "I need to become a trustworthy source. If I have a wife and child, suddenly my diapers are legit again. It's all about appearances."

"And what are you asking of me, exactly?" Emma asked.

"To be the face of that wife," he replied. "I'm asking you to enter into a business transaction. I need someone who can play the part of loving wife and I'm asking you to do it."

"But not for real?" She wasn't sure how to take this.

Emma had always planned on getting married and having children. It was one of her life dreams to be a mother and wife, but this wasn't the path she'd thought she take to get there. She'd always assumed it would be after a year or so of dating, and that there would be love involved.

"No. Not for real, although I do like you," Jackson replied. He handed her a wine glass.

"You said something about a child," she said, holding the glass but not sipping yet.

"Yes." He sat down in the kitchen chair next to her. "Having a wife isn't enough. I have to have a reason to use my own products."

Emma set her wine glass down. "Let me get this straight. You invited me out on this date to make sure we got along, and since we do, you're now asking me to marry you and have your child. To save your business."

"Yes," he agreed. "Though it sounds worse when you say it like that."

How else could it sound? she thought to herself. "You said this was a business deal, so what do I get out of doing this?"

"Money. You would be marrying a billionaire and having his child," Jackson explained. "You will never have bills again. You will live in the lap of luxury for the rest of your life. You and our child."

Emma didn't know how to respond. What was the appropriate response for that?

"Look at it this way," Jackson continued. "You want to be a marine biologist, right? There is no way that being a barista will get you there faster than I can."

She knew that it was the truth.

"I completely understand if you need some time to think about it," Jackson told her. "I know it's a big decision."

"Would we live together?" Emma asked, looking up from her untouched wine glass. "What does a future with you look like?"

"We would become a couple in public and I would propose," Jackson explained. "We would marry and have the wedding of your dreams. You would get pregnant as quickly as possible. You would live here, if you want. Or anywhere in the city you desire."

"And what about us?" Emma's throat tightened. She looked up at him, searching his handsome face for emotion.

"I like you," Jackson told her. His calm green eyes met hers. "I'm asking you to do this because, believe it or not, I trust you. We get along well and we have chemistry. I couldn't ask this of just anyone. You're special."

Emma swallowed hard. She sat there, unsure of what to do next.

"What are you thinking, Emma?" Jackson asked. His voice was soft.

"I'm... I'm not sure," Emma replied. Her brain was spinning. She hadn't expected this in a million years.

"If you need some time to think about it, you can have a couple of days," Jackson said. He placed his hand on top of hers. It was so warm and strong.

"I will need some time, please." She didn't pull her hand away. She liked the way it felt touching her. "It's kind of a big decision."

"I understand completely," he said, giving her hand a squeeze. "I'll answer any questions you might have. Here is the complete packet. I have a lawyer on retainer that you may utilize for any questions."

"Wouldn't that be a conflict of interest?" Emma asked, looking up at him. "Wouldn't he want the best deal for you?"

Jackson smiled. "He's hired to get you the best deal. I'm paying his fee indirectly. You are his client, not me."

"Oh, okay. I'm not sure what to even ask at the moment," Emma told him. "It's a lot to think about."

"Of course," Jackson agreed. "Would you like to stay here? You're welcome to spend the night."

She considered it. Despite it all, she still wasn't wearing panties and he had her wanting to go to bed with him. Maybe that was part of why she shouldn't stay. She wanted him.

"I'd actually like to go home, please," Emma told him. It wasn't that the sexual attraction wasn't there, because he was still sexy as hell, but rather that she wasn't sure she'd make good decisions if she stayed.

She needed to step back and think about what this would mean. As much as she had fantasized about being with Mr. Weathers, the actuality of really doing it was something entirely else.

"My driver will take you home," Jackson told her. He

pressed something on his phone to notify the driver. "But, like I said, you're more than welcome here."

"Thank you," Emma replied. She was suddenly very tired and this decision felt way too big. It was a good thing she didn't have to work tomorrow.

"Here's my private number," he said, handing her a card. "Call me anytime. Text me any questions. I want this to work with you. I think we can both be very happy with this. I know it's not the traditional method, but I think it can work out."

"I just need some time," Emma told him, standing from the table. "I'll let you know my decision in a couple of days. I'll need to speak with the lawyer."

"Of course, Emma." Jackson smiled at her. It made her heart thump in her chest when he looked at her like that. She was tempted to say yes to him right there with that smile.

"Thank you," was what she said instead.

He stood up and kissed her cheek. His lips were soft and he smelled so damn good she nearly changed her mind. She wanted to rip his clothes off and lick his skin and see if he smelled that good everywhere.

But, she needed to think critically. This needed to be a rational choice, not one made because she was horny.

He hovered with his mouth inches from hers, waiting for her to choose what to do next. She wanted to believe he wanted her as much as she did him. That this attraction wasn't just in her mind. She took a deep breath, and stepped away.

"I'll let you know my decision," she said, watching him. His green eyes shone with desire and lust clearly painted her face. She wanted to stay.

Luckily, there was a knock on the door, giving her a chance to look away. Jackson opened it to reveal a driver. She hurried away from Jackson and his bed, needing to think and wonder.

What would it be like to marry Jackson Weathers?

CHAPTER 7

mma

Should she marry a man for money?

The question floated around Emma's mind the moment she woke up.

No. I shouldn't, she decided as she made her coffee. *I should marry someone I love. I should keep dating, despite my lack of success, and it'll happen. I still have a few years before I need to worry about the biological clock.*

She sipped her coffee, pleased with her decision for a whole thirty seconds.

Yes, I should, she decided as she ate her cereal. She liked Jackson. He made her smile and she could see a future with him. Plus, the money from being his wife would make her dream job come true. She could work with any marine animal she pleased. She could buy the freaking marine park.

She took a shower, mulling over the pros and cons.

No, I shouldn't. I should love the man I have a child with. That was always the plan.

Yes, I should. Jackson would love the child and provide for it unconditionally. This child would be better cared for than most children in the world. She would have all the best child care development, nannies and staff.

By lunch, she'd changed her mind twelve times and was no closer to making a decision than she was when she first woke up.

She needed someone to talk her through it, but the NDA was going to be an issue.

She sighed and flopped herself on the couch. This wasn't a decision she could make on her own. For the millionth time that morning, Emma wished her mom was around so she could talk to her. Her mom would know just the right thing to say.

Emma closed her eyes and imagined her mother's face. She remembered the way her mom would smooth the hair back on her forehead and then kiss the bare skin. She'd always felt safe when her mother did that. She'd give anything for that feeling right now.

Her phone chimed. She was half afraid to look at it because it could be Jackson demanding an answer. It had only been less than a day, but she knew this was important. She wanted to make a decision as much as he probably wanted one.

She picked up her phone and let out a small sigh of relief. It wasn't him. It was Grace.

Hey! Want to get lunch? My appointment got canceled, so I'm baby free and hungry!

Emma played with the phone in her hands. Who better to talk to than a mother? Grace would have insight into what it took to raise a child. A plan started to form in Emma's mind.

Sure! How about the Indian food place on third?

Grace texted back a thumbs up with a see you in fifteen minutes! Emma quickly hopped off the couch and got her things together before heading out the door to meet her friend.

Grace waved from a table as Emma arrived. The restaurant wasn't terribly crowded yet as the lunch buffet had just started. The mouthwatering scents of curry and vegetables filled Emma's nose as she hurried over to sit with her friend.

"I ordered you a chai," Grace told her as Emma sat down.

"Thanks," Emma said with a smile. "Let's grab our food. I want to ask you a question when we sit back down."

The stood up and headed over to the buffet. Emma's stomach rumbled.

"I am actually really glad my appointment was moved," Grace admitted as they picked up their plates and began selecting from the appetizing options. "I'm so hungry and I needed a break. Sammy didn't sleep again last night."

"Poor little guy," Emma said, picking up a piece of naan bread. "Teeth again?"

"I'm not sure. He's just not a good sleeper in general," Grace told her. "But, did I tell you that he took his first step? Oh my god, it was amazing!"

"He did? My little walker!" Emma cooed.

"I'm so proud of him." Grace's face glazed over with pride as she thought about her little boy. "It's terrible, but I miss him already. It's crazy with kids how you can't wait to get away, but the minute they're gone, you miss them like crazy."

Emma nodded. She finished filling up her plate and went back to her seat. Her chai tea was nowhere to be seen yet. It was very different service than the night before.

"You said you had a question," Grace said, settling into her chair.

"I saw this job offer on an online forum I'm in, and I wanted to hear your thoughts," Emma said. She was going to keep this vague enough that the NDA wouldn't be an issue.

"Sure. Is it legit? There's so many scams out there right now," Grace replied, picking up her fork.

"I'll check, but I was more interested in your opinion on it. It's all hypothetical," Emma said. She took a deep breath. "The job is for a respected businessman from Canada. He needs a wife to stay here legally."

"So, you'd marry him and he'd get a green card and you get money?" Grace asked.

"Yeah. Sure." It was close enough to the truth.

Grace thought about it for a moment. "So, it's definitely in the gray area. It would really depend on the guy."

"Hot. Super hot. And a good guy," Emma told her. "Hypothetically."

"I guess I don't have an issue with it," Grace said slowly. "But is it really what you want? You want a family. Kids."

"What if kids were a possibility?" Emma held her breath waiting for Grace to answer.

"Ooh boy." Grace paused and gave it some serious thought as she chewed on her naan bread. "It still really depends on the guy. Is he going to be a good father? Is he financially sound?"

"Yes. He's got enough money to provide for me and a kid," Emma explained. "Plus, he's sweet, smart, and funny."

"What's the downside?" Grace asked. "There has to be a downside or he'd already be married."

"He's a womanizer."

"Like your boss? What's his name... Jackson Weathers?" Grace asked.

Emma nearly choked on her food. "He's not my boss. He just owns the building. And this has nothing to do with him. This is a totally different guy." Grace raised her eyebrows and Emma realized she'd probably said that with a little too much emphasis. Emma continued. "Would you marry a man like that? Have a baby? And know that there isn't love and he's probably going to cheat on you at some point? But, be super duper rich."

Grace thought for a moment. Emma really appreciated that her friend was giving this serious consideration, even though it was supposedly just a hypothetical idea.

"There are a lot of loveless marriages in the world. There are a lot of kids with no resources," Grace said after a moment. "Is it so bad to marry for money? No. There are way worse things in the world."

"So, I should do it?"

"Off of an internet ad? No fucking way, Emma!" Grace frowned at her. "You're smarter than that. Never do anything that involves sex on the internet."

Emma nodded. "But, if it weren't the internet, if it was a real thing, you'd take it?"

"If someone said I could have Sam and the money to hire three nannies, I'd take it in a heartbeat." Grace shrugged. "You know that little boy is the breath in my lungs. I'd do anything to have him."

"So would I," Emma agreed quietly. She'd seen the bond between Grace and her son. She craved that bond.

But would it be worth living with Jackson?

"Besides, if the guy in the ad really is that rich, who cares if he's messing around?" Grace said. "If it's not part of the contract, get yourself a pool boy and enjoy life. If he can, then you most certainly can, too."

"Equal opportunity cheating, huh?" Emma asked.

"Damn straight." Grace laughed. "You ready for more food?"

"You go on ahead. I still have some to finish."

"Okay. I'll grab you more bread," Grace said, getting up and leaving Emma with her half-eaten food.

Emma played with a grain of rice on her plate. Grace more or less said it was a good idea. Emma wasn't sure if that endorsement now helped or hurt.

If Emma agreed to this, she could have everything she'd ever wanted. She'd have money, kids, and opportunity to follow her dreams. It was so much more than she had right now as a slightly higher than minimum wage coffee worker.

Plus, Jackson Weathers was a lot of fun to be around. He was hotter than sin. Making a baby with him would be pretty amazing. Plus, she could see them at least being friends. It would be a better relationship than many marriages she'd seen.

"I'll do it," she whispered to herself.

She waited thirty seconds, but didn't change her mind. This time, the decision was sticking.

"Okay," she said to the empty table. "I guess I'm going to marry Jackson Weathers."

CHAPTER 8

Jackson Weathers paced the floor of his office. For the second time this week, he was nervous and it drove him crazy.

Emma was on her way up to see him. She'd told him that she'd made her decision and was coming to speak to him about it.

And now he was terrified she was going to say no.

He'd been pleasantly surprised by how much fun he'd had on their date. It was something that he'd done hundreds of times, but she made it fresh and fun. He loved that she actually enjoyed eating and could hold a conversation that wasn't entirely about herself or celebrity gossip.

And that kiss. He'd taken three cold showers to deal with the feelings that popped up each time he thought of that kiss.

She was something special and he could only hope that she was going to come up here and say yes.

He wasn't sure what he'd do if she turned him down.

A timid knock on the door drew his attention.

"Come in," he said, hoping it didn't sound too forceful. He didn't want to scare her away.

Her dark hair peeked into the room followed by bright hazel eyes. She smiled as she opened the door and walked the rest of the way in.

She wore a smart business suit. It was obviously well worn, but it fit her well. The gray material hugged her curves and he found himself wishing that the demure hem of the skirt was about six inches higher.

It was everything he could do not to grab her and take her right there on his desk.

"Mr. Weathers, I'm here to discuss your offer," she said, sounding like she had practiced the line several times. It was rather endearing.

"Please come in," he greeted her. He pulled out a chair for her to sit and hurried around to sit at his desk. "I'm anxious to hear your reply."

She settled into the chair, taking her time. She was making him wait and they both knew it. His foot bounced under the desk as he watched her cleavage rise with every nervous breath.

"So, what did you decide?" Jackson asked, keeping his voice light.

"After much consideration, I have decided to accept your offer, provided you make some changes." She handed him a thick stack of papers and crossed her legs. She sat up perfectly straight and held herself with the cool confidence of a lawyer.

"What kind of changes?" he asked, flipping over the first page of the document and looking through it.

"First, I want one more date before I officially accept. I want to make sure that we have the right kind of chemistry to make this work."

"I don't think chemistry is an issue," he told her, but she didn't change her expression. "But, another date to confirm that this is a good partnership is a fine. Done."

"Good. I want you to plan it."

"That should have been mentioned before I agreed," he scolded gently. She kept her head up. Likely her lawyer told her to do this to put him off balance. "But, I still agree."

"Good. Second, I want my own place. I want it in your building." She swallowed hard, stopping herself before she could say too much. Her lawyer had coached her well.

"That may be difficult," he said, drawing this out a little bit. "The building is in high demand."

She opened her mouth, stopped, and raised her chin. "That is your problem to figure out. It's something I want. My own residence in your building."

With a little more practice, she would become an excellent negotiator, he thought with a smile.

"I'll see what I can do."

"No, you'll do it." She swallowed hard again, her eyes just a little too wide. He didn't want to torment her, so he didn't do his usual bargaining tactics. He wanted to give her everything, not destroy her. It was a strange feeling.

"Okay. It'll be done." He smiled. "Anything else?"

"One last thing," she said. Her voice quavered slightly. "I want something else. I want a house outside of the city once we have kids. And I want you to be there most of the time."

"You want me to commute to the city?" he asked, not liking this last amendment.

She nodded. "I want you to be important in your child's life. But a kid needs room to run. They need parks and play space, and while there are some in the city, it's nothing like having a house with a yard. And a dog."

"You want a dog, too?" he asked, raising one eyebrow. "Is that one of the changes?"

"Eventually." She licked her lips before biting the lower one.

She didn't know it, but doing that would get her just about anything. When she bit her lower lip, his mind went south. He instinctively knew it was the kind of thing she would do when she was going to orgasm and his brain couldn't focus on anything else.

"I'll talk to my lawyer," he said, forcing himself to tear his eyes away from her mouth. "It wouldn't be a problem until the child is at least a year old, right? So, there's time."

She chewed her cheek and then nodded. "So, you agree to my amendments?"

He looked her over, taking in her professional suit and the quiet femininity to her. She really was going to be perfect for this.

"Yes," he told her after a moment. "I'll have the lawyers draw up the final agreement and we'll get signatures on it."

She let out a nervous breath as she smiled. "But, we get another date. I want to make sure that we really do get along well. I'm not expecting us to fall madly in love or anything, but I would like to make sure that we can be friends."

He smiled. "That's better than a lot of marriages I've seen," he agreed.

She nodded. "So, I guess that's it? I'm not really used to negotiations. What am I supposed to do now?"

"I would advise a hearty handshake and something about setting up another meeting with my secretary," he advised.

"Okay." She stood up and offered him her hand. "Thank you, Mr. Weathers. I'll have my attorney set up another meeting to make sure everything is finalized."

"That's perfect," he told her, taking her hand in his. She was small and delicate in his hand and so warm. She flushed, her cheeks and throat turning red. Her chest started to color as well and he wondered just how far south the coloring went.

He realized he was still holding her hand and quickly released her. She smiled and glanced around his office.

"Oh, I have a question for you," he said, not wanting her to leave. "Do you like to sail?"

"I've never actually ever gone sailing. It looks like fun, though."

"Okay. I think I have an idea for our date," he replied. "I'll pick you up tonight." He loved that she grinned.

"I'll see you then. Thank you for your time," she said, obviously trying to keep her professional image going. She managed to hold it for a second longer, then bolted for the door.

He stared at the empty room, feeling a little pang of loss from her leaving and yet smiling at the same time. She was adorable, sweet, and had no idea the exciting effect she had on his libido. He was already excited for their next date.

 _mma_

Emma had everything ready to go, but she did one last final mental check just to be sure. She wanted to make sure this date was perfect. She needed it to be perfect, or she wasn't sure she could go through with this.

She liked Jackson. She _really_ liked him, but this marriage idea felt so forced. It felt fast and cheap because they weren't going to marry for love. They were marrying for business. Granted, she was going to get everything she ever wanted: money, a house, a baby, and the opportunity to follow her dreams, but at what cost? Would it be worth giving up on love?

She tugged at her dark ponytail. _Was this something she could really do?_

She looked at herself in the mirror, taking in her long dark hair, the green swirled through light brown of her eyes, and the slight notch in her nose.

Who was she? Was she the type of woman to do this?

This date was going to be the deciding factor. If it went well, if she thought that they could be friends as well as lovers, she would say yes. She would sign the contract and marry him. For the amount of money and lifestyle she was going to get, she could put up with a lot worse.

Still, her conscience nagged at her. Their marriage would be a sham. Their child would be a publicity stunt. Was this really what she wanted?

"Just be yourself and see what happens," she told the mirror. He would be here any second. She zipped up the light windbreaker over her t-shirt and capri pants. He told her to dress comfortably. The weather would be cooler out on the water, so even though it was summer and hot outside, she should bring a coat and hat.

The doorbell to her apartment rang. She gave herself one last nod in the mirror and went to answer it.

She opened the door expecting to see a driver or someone to pick her up. She wasn't expecting to find Jackson standing there with a dozen roses and a box of chocolates.

"These are for you," he said, handing them off with a smile.

"You didn't have to get these," she told him, lowering her face to the flowers and breathing in their sweet scent. It had been a long time since anyone had brought her flowers.

"I wanted to." His green eyes were soft as he looked at her. "You deserve them."

"I'm going to put these in some water," she said, feeling a blush heat her cheeks as she stepped back and let him inside. "Do I need to bring anything for our date?"

"Just yourself." He carefully closed the door behind him and looked around her apartment.

She tried not to feel self-conscious as she hurried to the kitchen and filled a vase with water for the flowers. She liked her apartment, but it wasn't exactly the place she'd bring a billionaire. Sure, it was tiny and she probably should pick up more, but it was hers and she was happy with it.

"Okay. I'm ready," she announced, hurrying back to him. He hadn't left the entry area. She opened the front door. "After you. I have to lock up."

He stepped out into the warm afternoon sunshine and she quickly locked the door behind them. Her hands shook with nerves, and she did her best to hide it.

She led the way out of her building to the parking lot where a bright blue sports car sat waiting for them.

"What happened to the red one?" Emma asked.

Jackson looked confused for a moment before chuckling. "Oh. I just felt like taking this one."

"Oh. Okay." Emma nodded. That was fine. Perfectly normal. Everyone had to choose between two hundred-thousand dollar cars on a regular basis.

He held the passenger door open for her. She wasn't sure how it was possible, but this car was even nicer than the last one. She wondered if she should take off her shoes to help keep the interior clean. It felt wrong to use the car like a regular vehicle. It felt like using a Monet painting as a coaster.

Jackson kept up an easy, friendly conversation as they left her apartment building and drove to the marina. He drove fast, pushing the car more than Emma would have. She tried not to look at the road as he drove, instead focusing on him.

She knew he was a good driver, but he took far more risks than she did as a driver.

He pulled to a stop and put in the code at the marina gate. She'd seen the boats out on the water, but she'd never been out on one. Boats cost money and that was one thing she didn't have.

If you marry him, you can be on a boat anytime you want, she thought to herself. She shook her head. Tonight wasn't about falling in love with his money. Tonight was about making sure that they were a good fit.

Jackson parked the car and ran around to open her door for her. It was a simple gesture, but it felt nice. It made her feel taken care of. Wanted.

"You said you've never been sailing, so I thought I would take you," Jackson explained, leading her down to the pier.

Docked along the side was a beautiful sailboat. Emma had no knowledge on sailing other than pirates did it, but she could tell this boat was nice. It wasn't the biggest in the marina, but it had something to it that told her it was probably the most expensive sailboat there.

"Her name is the Techno Volante," he said, guiding her to the gangplank. "Welcome aboard."

"Do I need to call you Captain?" Emma asked, carefully putting her foot on the gangplank. The boat bobbed slightly and she was glad she was watching what she was doing.

"Only if you want to," he replied. He winked at her, nearly causing her to lose her balance. "I like to be called Captain."

She grinned and stepped onto the boat. "This is beautiful," she said, looking around. Everything was wood paneled or shimmering white. She could see three neatly hung sails, ready to take them on an adventure.

"I'm glad you like it," Jackson said, coming up behind her. "I thought we could sail today. If you'd rather take the yacht, we can, but it needs a crew. This boat I can handle by myself. I thought you'd prefer the intimacy."

The word intimacy made her cheeks flush. She could go for some intimacy. Hell yes.

"I like this boat," she said, her voice husky. "We can do it on the yacht next time."

He grinned at her words and she flushed straight down to

her toes. "If you say so," he replied. He moved past her, his hand on her shoulder as he passed.

"You know what I meant," she stuttered.

"Sure do," he called back, heading to the front of the boat to untie the ropes.

She rolled her eyes and shook her head. There was no recovering that one. Best to just move on.

"Can I help?" she asked, coming over to where he was working with a rope.

"You want to steer us out of the marina?" he asked.

"I don't have a sailing license," she told him. "Just a driving license."

He laughed. "That will work. This way."

He brought her to the back of the open boat to a large steering wheel. It looked exactly like what she thought a pirate would use to steer his ship. She put both hands on the wheel and braced her feet.

"I'll get us started. We have to use the engine until we're in open water," he explained, turning a key in the ignition. The boat rumbled to life and she felt her palms go sweaty. "Slow and steady."

Jackson stood behind her, putting his strong hands on her shoulders. She had to focus on what they were doing and not the fact that he was touching her. It was a difficult task to ignore the heat he caused.

He gave simple directions, keeping his voice low and calm as she worked the boat out of the marina. It was like driving her uncle's giant Buick, but on steroids. She managed to get out of the marina without hitting anything or tipping the boat over, which she considered a true success.

Jackson cut the engine and they gradually came to a stop, or at least what felt like a stop. It was hard to tell if they were actually going anywhere with the way the waves constantly moved around them.

"Excellent job," Jackson told her, giving her shoulders a gentle squeeze. His praise meant the world to her.

"Is it always this... bumpy?" Emma asked. Everything was in motion. The boat went up and down. It went side to side. It went diagonally up and down and side to side at the same time. Nothing felt secure.

"This is actually pretty calm," Jackson told her. He ran around to various ropes, loosening and tightening different ones to make the sails come down. They flapped in the wind.

"Calm?" She swallowed hard. Now that she wasn't focused on not crashing the boat, she was very aware of her stomach and just how unhappy it was. "This doesn't feel calm."

Jackson looked over at her. "You might be getting seasick," he said. His green eyes watched her with concern. "Do you get motion sickness?"

"Only when I read in the car," she said. Her stomach knotted and she swallowed down, her mouth too wet and too dry at the same time.

"Look out at the horizon," Jackson coached. He unfurled another sail. "Let's see if some air helps."

He did something more with the sails, but Emma wasn't paying attention. Her focus was on the bobbing horizon and trying to keep her stomach under control. She heard him go to the big steering wheel and the boat moved even more. She tried not to groan.

A fresh breeze hit her face. It helped a little and she opened her eyes. *Maybe I can do this*, she thought.

And then she threw up over the side.

Three times in a row.

She didn't even think she had that much in her stomach. It felt like she was bringing up dinners from last week. It was unstoppable.

I'm making a great impression, she thought as she lost last Tuesday's dinner over the side of the boat.

She vaguely noticed Jackson coming to her side. He helped hold her hair back out of her face. He rubbed her back and made soft noises.

Finally, her body stopped. The nausea was still there, but there was nothing left to throw up. She felt like curling up into a ball and dying.

"How you doing?" he asked, still rubbing small circles onto her back.

"Do you have any water?" she asked, her voice raw. She kept her eyes closed and pressed her head against the metal railing, grateful that it was cold.

She heard him take a few steps before coming back with a bottle of water. She sipped at it gingerly, not wanting to give her stomach anything but still wanting to get the taste out of her mouth.

"Thanks," she mumbled.

Jackson stood there for a moment, watching her.

"Get me the speeder," Jackson said. Emma turned and looked at him, confused. He had his phone to his ear. "Set up the island house... Yes, the island house. Yes, I know. Do it."

He hung up the phone and put it in his pocket.

"What's that about?" she asked, keeping her voice low. She felt like if she opened her mouth too wide or spoke too loudly, her stomach would rebel again.

"Just changing plans," Jackson replied. He rubbed her back again. "In hindsight, we should have taken the yacht."

"Or maybe just stayed on land," Emma agreed. "If we get divorced, at least you don't have to worry about me taking the boats."

Jackson chuckled. "I'm not sure if that should make me optimistic or worried," he replied.

She swallowed hard as a wave knocked them around.

"I'm going to point us into the wind," Jackson told her. "Are you okay for a minute?"

"I promise not to fall off the boat," she said, clutching her stomach. "Other than that, I guarantee nothing."

Concern filled his face as he moved quickly to the various ropes and changed the way the sails hung. She appreciated that he was trying to help her, but every bob of the boat just made things worse. She decided that she hated sailing.

The sound of an engine caught her attention. The last she'd looked, they were the only boat as far as she could see. She cracked open one eye and saw a speed boat coming in. It was headed straight for them.

The speedboat came up alongside the sailboat and tossed Jackson a line.

"You made good time," Jackson said to the man driving the speedboat.

"You said right away, sir," the man replied.

"You good to take the Techno back to the marina?" Jackson asked the man.

"Yes, sir." The man nodded. "I also took the liberty of informing the chef. She's moved things around to make it easier for you."

Jackson thanked the man and came over to Emma. "Can you walk?" he asked her. His voice was low and comforting.

"I think so," Emma whispered. "Why?"

"We're going to get you off this boat," Jackson told her. "Fred will sail back and we'll take the speed boat back to land. I don't want you to be miserable."

"But our date," Emma protested.

"Our date should be fun," Jackson told her. "This is not fun. Come on."

He took her in his arms. He felt so strong and steady that for a moment, she felt just a little bit better. Carefully, with the help of Fred, she made her way off the sailboat and into the speedboat. She wasn't quite sure how changing one boat for another was going to help, but she was willing to do anything to feel better at this point.

Jackson exchanged some words with Fred before hopping in the driver's seat. He made sure that Emma was as comfortable as she could be before turning on the engine and pulling away from his sailboat.

The speedboat was a vast improvement over the sailboat. With the extra speed and the wind in her face, she started to feel better. The motion of the waves was far less in this boat. They were going so fast that it felt more like a car. A car drive she could handle.

Slowly, she sat up. They weren't heading in the direction she thought the marina was. They weren't even heading in the direction she thought land was.

"Where are we going?" she asked, looking around.

Jackson looked over at her. "To dinner. If you're ready."

"As long as it's not on water."

He grinned and pushed the boat to go faster.

mma

The sun hung above the horizon, shimmering with gold and scarlet as an island came into view. She had never been more happy to see solid ground in her life. For the first time, she understood why sailors always sounded so relieved to shout, "land ho!" She certainly felt like shouting it.

Her stomach had calmed down since getting on the speedboat. She still wasn't ready to eat a large meal, but she no longer felt like the world was trying to throw her off of it either. Emma mentally crossed off a sailing career as a future occupation.

Jackson pulled the boat up onto the beach. The coarse sand grated against the hull of the ship as he made sure the boat was high enough on the beach not to get pulled out into the ocean with the tide.

Jackson took a deep breath and turned to her.

"I wasn't planning on bringing you here. So, nothing's

ready. I had thought we'd sail to the yacht and eat there, but I don't think you on a boat is a good idea for the rest of the evening."

"I would very much agree," she told him.

He hesitated, and ran his hand through his hair. "I don't want you to get the wrong idea," he said. "The house here is small. It's not really for guests."

"You're worried I won't be impressed?" she asked.

"Yes." He shrugged. "The goal was to impress you tonight. So far, I'm not doing very well."

"Says who?" Emma countered. "I'm excited to see it."

"Okay. Just know that it isn't my best property."

"It's an island. I'm impressed." Emma smiled at him and looked up to see a man hurrying toward them. The man wore a plain windbreaker and jeans, and had a bright smile.

"Mr. Weathers, you're early," the man said, coming up to the boat. He tipped his head to Emma. "Everything is set up in the house. I'm afraid it's not perfect, but I did the best I could in the time given."

"I understand, Jeb. Thank you."

Jackson hopped out of the speed boat and offered Emma his hand. She took it, carefully getting out of the boat. Dry land felt amazing under her feet. She wondered if she should kiss the ground, she was so glad to no longer be on a boat.

She wasn't sure how she was going to get home, but for the moment, she wasn't going to worry about it. She'd figure out what to do in a few hours. Maybe there was a bridge that she could take to get home. Anything but a boat. Or, she would simply live on the island forever if she had to get back on a boat to leave. It was a sacrifice she was willing to make.

Jackson held out his hand for her. "This way," he said with a smile. "Jeb will take care of the boat."

She took Jackson's hand and walked with him along the

beach. His touch made her skin tingle. She liked it. She liked being with him.

"Where are we going?" she asked as they hiked up the beach. Trees obscured most of her vision.

"Dinner at my place," he replied. He stopped short. "As long as you'd like dinner. If your stomach is still queasy, we can do something else."

She smiled. "My stomach is feeling better. I'll just eat light and I think I'll be okay. Thank you."

He looked her over and then nodded. He gave her hand a squeeze before continuing up the hill.

She liked that he was concerned. She felt a little bad that she'd messed up his plans for a romantic date night with her seasickness. This obviously wasn't the way he had planned things. Yet, he was taking it in stride and still smiling.

As they crested the ridge of the hill, she saw the house. It was beautiful. Giant windows overlooked the ocean on all sides. The building itself was probably only a bedroom and main room, but the windows more than made up for the lack of space inside. She grinned and picked up her pace.

Jackson lead her to the front door. He didn't knock, instead going right inside. The house was even more beautiful on the inside than it was outside. Soft, comfortable furniture in grays and off-whites sat on gray driftwood colored floors. The windows were like being inside a bubble looking out at the world.

"Wow," she whispered, taking off her shoes at the door. She didn't want to track sand inside. "What is this place?"

"This is my personal beach house," Jackson explained. "Since you mentioned you wanted a house with space, I thought you might like it here. It's one of my favorite places to come and relax. Plus, it was close."

"It's amazing," she agreed, walking through the home. It

was as small as she suspected, but warm and inviting. She loved it.

"Let me get you a drink," Jackson said, dropping her hand as he went to the small kitchen. "Have a seat. Or, feel free to freshen up."

The room had a large comfortable looking couch and several smaller chairs. A wood burning fireplace sat off to the side and Emma could only imagine how comfortable this room must be in the winter with a fire lighting up the big windows.

Pictures hung on the far wall by the window. She walked over and looked them over. They were all of Jackson in various locations around the world. He climbed mountains, she learned, looking at the pictures.

She went to the small bathroom off to the side and cleaned herself up. Her makeup was smudged from crying and her hair tangled in every imaginable direction. She scrubbed at her teeth with her fingers and did her best to make herself look presentable before going back out to the main room.

The sun started to set, painting the entire room in gold and orange. Emma stood in front of a window, absorbing the color of the setting sun with her entire being. Her stomach queasiness was completely gone now. Solid ground had done the trick.

"Here you are," Jackson said, handing her a heavy glass full of amber liquid.

Emma sniffed before sipping. The taste was ginger ale.

"Is there any alcohol in this?" she asked, taking a deeper sip.

"No, just ginger. I thought it might help your stomach."

She smiled and took another sip. It was sweet of him to make sure she was feeling better.

"I smell something cooking. Are we eating here?"

Jackson nodded. "I have shrimp mosca. It's my favorite. I'm afraid it's not done, since we had to move it from the yacht. I figured you wouldn't want to eat on the water."

"No," Emma agreed. Just the thought being on the boat again made her stomach tense. She took another sip of ginger ale.

"It's just us here, so we'll have to mostly fend for ourselves. I'm afraid I only have Jeb and some security on the island right now."

"Jeb was the man who took the speed boat on the beach, right?" Emma asked, recalling the name.

Jackson smiled at her. "Yes. He maintains the island for me. When our plans changed, he set up our dinner here instead of out on the yacht like I had planned."

"Thank you for changing your plans," Emma said. "I'm sorry about my stomach."

Jackson took her hands in his. "Don't be sorry, Emma. This may work out better."

"Still, I know you had everything all planned. I feel a little bad."

"Part of being a business owner is the ability to change. To make things work even if they aren't quite the plan. Now, you get to see my favorite place in the world. This is my sanctuary. I don't let just anyone here."

"You don't?" Emma asked. "Is that what you tell all the girls?"

Jackson shook his head. "You are the first woman I've ever brought here," he admitted. "I know that sounds like a great line, but it isn't. This place is special to me. It's mine. No one knows about it."

He looked around the room with soft eyes and Emma had no reason to doubt him.

"Thank you for sharing this with me."

He squeezed her hands. "We're supposed to share every-thing, right? Besides, it felt right to bring you here."

Warmth blossomed in her chest. He was going to give this marriage a real go. This wasn't just all business to him. He wanted to make it work with her.

She made the decision to officially say yes right then. It wasn't the fancy boat, the nice meal, or the house. It was that he was sharing it with her. He was opening up his world to her, giving her the chance to really be a part of his life.

That made the contract something she could do.

"Let me show you the kitchen," Jackson said. "Dinner isn't quite ready yet, but the sunset view is the best from in there."

He pulled on her hand, giddy like a child showing her a prized possession. She grinned, following quickly behind him. He brought her around a corner into a beautiful stain-less steel kitchen. It wasn't big, but it was all state of the art.

Something simmered on the stove-top that smelled abso-lutely divine. Her mouth started watering.

"Take a seat anywhere. I just need to set up a few things," he said, going to the sink and washing his hands. He picked up a wooden spoon. "I have shrimp, Italian bread, a salad, and some dessert."

"That sounds amazing," she told him, walking into the kitchen. The scent of rosemary and wine hung in the air and she breathed it in deeply.

"I had more planned."

"I appreciate this," she said, coming close to him.

Now that her mind was made up, she wasn't nervous. This felt right. She went up on tiptoes and kissed his lips.

It was a small kiss. Just a peck, yet it sent shock waves through her core.

Jackson froze, his eyes going wide. He tipped his head, wanting to ask the question. Was she saying yes to him?

"Yes," she told him. "My answer is yes. And it's not the house that did it. It was you."

He blinked twice before a slow smile bloomed. He set down his wooden spoon and put his hands on either side of her face. His eyes filled her vision as he looked her over. She loved that his pupils dilated as he looked at her.

And then he kissed her.

On a scale of one to ten, this kiss was a fifteen. Sweet, sensual, sexy, spicy, and so much more. She couldn't come up with the words to describe the kiss.

"How about we wait on dinner?" she whispered, suddenly filled with a different kind of hunger.

He grinned and kissed her again, reaching behind him and turning the stove-top to low.

 ackson

Jackson wrapped his arms around Emma, loving the way she seemed to fit so perfectly in them. She was made for him. He kissed her fiercely, tasting her sweetness as they stumbled from the kitchen and out into the living room.

Her kisses were sweeter than wine. Maybe it was just his imagination or the fact that she had agreed to be his, but he'd never had better. His hands itched to feel her skin, to take her as his. To make their agreement official in the most primal of ways.

She pulled away, shedding her windbreaker and hat. She wore cute capri pants that showed off the curve of her calves and a cute t-shirt. It wasn't supposed to be sexy, but Jackson couldn't think of anything he'd rather see more.

His hands rubbed up and down her shirt, eager to find their way to her skin eventually. He rubbed his hand up to the back of her neck, where he pulled her in closer for his kiss. His tongue darted inside her mouth, and she responded with short gasps of pleasure.

"Come with me," he whispered, grabbing her hand and pulling her to the bedroom. She deserved a bed for their first time. He wanted to do this right.

The bedroom was small and peaceful. The big windows were open to the ocean, and the sky was now dark and starting to twinkle with stars. The lights of the city were tiny dots on the horizon. They were alone out here.

He kissed her again, reveling in her taste. He wanted to take this slow, to enjoy himself, but at the same time the desire within him couldn't wait. He wanted to claim her as his without another second passing.

He took control of his lust, letting it fire through him but not take over.

She on the other hand, wasn't waiting. She pushed him to the bed, and mounted him, putting her legs on either side of his hips. He grinned. This was even better.

She leaned forward, kissing him as his fingers traced up her back. It wasn't hard to lift the thin t-shirt and pull it up over her head. She smiled at him as it cleared her head and she shook her glorious dark hair around her shoulders.

She was perfect. The bra was white and fit her tits to perfection. Her skin was smooth and flawless, pale against the dark of her hair. She bit her lip, drawing the red lower lip into her mouth.

She shivered as his fingers caressed the top of her breast. The skin was so smooth and soft he could barely stand it. She closed her eyes and he touched her. Every breath made her chest rise and fall beneath his finger tips.

"So beautiful," he whispered.

At that, her eyes opened and looked at him. A slow smile filled her face at the compliment. She leaned forward and kissed him, pressing her chest into his. He wanted the bra out of the way. With experienced fingers, he undid the snaps and pulled the fabric away.

She sat back, letting him look at her. He didn't want to just look. He reached for her, pulling her chest to his mouth. He licked one nipple and then the other, feeling the nipple contract under his tongue. She moaned with the sensation and shivered against him with delight.

Her hips moved, arching and writhing against him. Already, he could feel the pressure rising within him. He was still a long ways off, but the effect her movement had on him was heady.

He wanted the clothing gone.

He sat up and flipped her onto the bed. She shrieked with surprise, but didn't fight him. If anything, her eyes grew darker.

He tugged at her waistband, pulling the capri pants down and away from her legs. His fingers traced up the soft curve of her ankle, up her calf, along the sensitive skin of her inner thigh, and finally up to the lacy pair of panties.

She was already wet and his cock throbbed to feel her warmth. He wanted to dive into and take her as his own. Instead, he traced a finger along the damp line of her pussy. Her low moan told him that she wanted this as much as he did.

He tugged at the sides, and her breath caught. She looked up at him, her eyes shining with desire and moonlight as she lifted her hips and let him take the panties away. She lay there, spread out on the bed, awaiting him.

But her pleasure came first. He would get what he wanted in a moment. He could have that much self control for just a few minutes to make her come. He wanted to know how her face would twist. He wanted to know what little sounds she would make.

So he knelt on the floor, pulling her so her legs hung off the edge of the bed with him between them. Her breath came in small gasps, her muscles tight and her legs open.

He started slow, simply taking a long lick from the bottom of her to the top, careful not to give too much attention to her clit. He did a few more of these long, slow licks, and she was beginning to moan with the pleasure. The sound drove him wild, and he had to reach down and rub himself through his pants.

She gasped as he flicked his tongue against her now fully engorged clit. He sucked on it gently, before lifting the skin off of it and gently flicking his tongue on it. Her gasps and moans became more and more fevered, and she grabbed his hair and pulled, bringing him in closer. She tasted so good, he didn't care if she pulled on his hair.

He gladly continued licking her sweetness, until she started tensing up. He kept the same rhythm and intensity as she tensed up more and more, moaning louder and louder, until she arched her hips and let out a scream as an orgasm washed over her body. She bucked her hips again and again as her muscles spasmed and clenched in total bliss.

She panted his name, her fingers slowly letting go of him as she came down from her orgasm. He quickly pulled his shirt off and shed his pants.

Her eyes went to his chest and she licked her lips. She sat up, putting her hands on his chest.

"Let me," she whispered, her hands going down his chest to the waistband of his boxers. Her skin sent tingles of electricity straight down to his cock. He was half surprised his boxers hadn't split wide open from the strength of his erection.

She turned him on.

She hooked her fingers in his waistband and tugged. It

took her a moment to work the fabric down and around him, but then she stared with awe. Most women did.

She kissed him, pressing her hot skin against his. His cock searched for her opening, wanting to dive into her wet little pussy. It was the only thing he could concentrate on. He needed to know exactly how it felt to be inside of her.

Gently, he lowered her to the bed. This time, she was fully on it, not hanging with her feet off. She was so damn beautiful he felt like he could come right there, just looking at her. He wasn't some fresh little teenager with no experience. He'd been with countless women, but the woman in front of him right now drove him crazy with sudden lust.

He gave her a deep kiss, and as he pulled away she looked deep into his eyes. His first thought was to go and grab the condom, but they didn't need that. She was signing the contract. They were supposed to make a baby.

The tip of his cock found the hole it was looking for, and slowly began pressing forward. He rocked forward gently, moving deeper within her as slowly as he could tolerate. He'd forgotten how smooth a woman could be without a condom between them.

God, she felt amazing. She was heaven on earth. There was nothing but the two of them, joining completely. Nothing was in his way this time. There was no need for him to take any precautions. The freedom was exhilarating. He wanted to come right there, but closed his eyes and pushed himself to go further. He couldn't have her thinking he was a two-pump chump, even though it was her that was making him want to be.

She wrapped her arms around him, digging her nails slightly into her back. He filled her completely, loving the gasp of pleasure that escaped her perfect lips as he dove to the hilt.

Jackson loved the sensation of having his skin touch

every inch of hers. He lovingly kissed her shoulder while pushing himself deep inside of her. He squeezed her breast, playing with the nipple gently. She moaned softly, and soon she arched her head back, looking for a kiss. He was happy to oblige her, grabbing her under her chin and pulling her in for a kiss while thrusting again deep inside of her.

Her tongue found his, sweet and innocent. She moaned as he quested ever deeper inside of her, searching for contentment. Her moans spurred him on, urging to him to go faster and harder.

Beneath him, her breasts bounced and her hips rose to meet him. He'd never felt this turned on before. Every second that he held back, the pain of incredible pleasure called to him. All he could hear was Emma's voice, urging him to go harder and faster.

He gripped her hips, taking control. He needed to fill her. He needed to claim her as his own. It was no longer a conscious thought, but rather a primal instinct. Her body tightened around him, reacting with her own primal needs.

"Yes," she whispered, her eyes going wide as she felt him swell within her.

She contracted around him, milking him. If her first orgasm was powerful, the second was a tsunami. It washed over him, obliterating everything in its path. There was no mistake, no holding out.

The only thing he could do was come.

A rising tide flooded through his body, white lightning pouring out of him. He could feel himself about to lose it. She felt amazing, tight and wet. With a growl, he let himself go deep inside of her. She moaned with pleasure as his semen flooded into her, filling and coating her as she kept working his cock in her pussy. He groaned as he relaxed, his muscles twitching as he emptied the last of his semen into her. She kept dancing her ass against him, working the last drops of cum from deep within him.

He collapsed, pressing his face into the curve of her shoulder. How did she feel so damn perfect? How did she move in just the right way to drive him wild that easily? He'd meant to go longer. He'd wanted to show her exactly what he was capable of, but he just couldn't contain himself with her.

She was too much for him.

Beneath him, she sighed with contentment. Her hands traced lazy circles on his back as he stayed deep within her, relishing the feeling of having absolutely nothing between them.

"That was better than anything," she murmured. He grinned. At least he'd made her happy. He lifted his head to see her smile. Good lord, she was beautiful. He had certainly chosen the right woman.

"Are you ready for some dinner?" he asked.

"That means I have to get up," she replied. "I don't think I can move. You killed me."

He chuckled, letting her words stroke his ego. "You can eat naked."

She eyed him. "If I do that, can we do this again?"

He grinned. "Sure."

She sighed and relaxed back against the bed with a happy sound. He liked it and wanted her to always make that soft sound of contentment.

He carefully put his hands on either side of her and pushed up from the bed. She lay beneath him, perfect, soft and feminine. He was already getting hard again just looking at her and remembering how good she felt.

She slowly came to sitting, a soft frown crossing her face. "What?" he asked.

"I think we're going to have to stay here forever," she told him. "I feel so good right now." She looked over at him and her pupils dilated wide. "Plus, I'm not getting on a boat, so you're just going to have to stay here and have sex with me forever."

That actually didn't sound like a bad plan to Jackson.

"I could live with that," Jackson replied, offering her a hand to stand up. "All I'd have to do is cancel the helicopter."

"Wait, helicopter?" Emma asked.

"Unless you want to take the boat home."

She shook her head. "Nope. But, I'm not ready to leave yet."

He grinned. When he looked at her he felt like he could go all night. His animal brain already hummed with the desire to fill her with his seed again. He could barely wait. Maybe dinner could wait a little longer.

"Good," he said, pushing her back onto the bed. "Because I'm not done with you yet."

mma

The next few days after signing the contract were an absolute blur for Emma.

She quit her job. Movers came and boxed up everything she owned. She told her landlord she was moving. And suddenly she was living in Jackson's apartment building.

She had an apartment two floors below Jackson's penthouse suite. Her apartment was much, much, much smaller than Jackson's, but that was fine. It was for her, anyway. Not the two of them.

The movers put her furniture and clothing into the apartment almost exactly the way she'd had her old apartment set up. The only real difference was that now she had a much better view.

She was reorganizing her dishes when there came a knock on the door. She opened it, thinking it was the movers.

"You really should be more careful who you open the door to," Jackson teased. He stood in the hallway with fresh flowers as he leaned against the door frame looking cocky and sexy.

"I shouldn't let you in?" she asked, reaching for the flowers.

"You should let me in," he agreed. "But you didn't know it was me."

"Says you." She held open the door and went to put the flowers in a vase. These ones were pink roses and they somehow smelled even better than the ones from before. It took her a minute to locate her spare flower vase. If he kept bringing her flowers like this, she was going to run out of places to put them.

"What do you think of the apartment?" he asked her, looking around. "Do you want new furniture?"

"My furniture is fine," she told him. She arranged the flower stems to best show off the blossoms. "And the apartment is perfect. The elevator ride is about ten seconds and I have an amazing view."

She turned from the sink and smiled at him.

"Thank you," she said, taking a step toward him.

"I'm glad you like it," he replied. His green eyes watched her and although his mouth didn't smile, his eyes did. "I was hoping you might bring some of your things upstairs."

"Upstairs?" Emma asked, not quite understanding.

"I cleaned out a drawer for you," he replied. "We are supposed to look like we're moving in together."

"Right." Her heart fluttered. He had cleaned out a drawer. No one had ever done that for her. Even though it was all fake, it still felt like this was something important.

"Only if you want," he continued. "I don't want to push you."

"Let me grab some things," she told him. She grinned and

ran off to her new bedroom. It only took a moment to throw some socks, underthings, and pajamas into a bag. She added a comfortable skirt and some t-shirts so she could have something easy to wear. Even though it was only two floors down, she didn't want to do the walk of shame if she didn't have to.

"That's it?" Jackson asked when he saw her small bag. She had actually taken out a sweater thinking it might be too much.

"For the first trip," she told him. She wasn't sure just how big the drawer was. If she had space, she would bring up more. It wasn't like she had to go far.

"Okay." He smiled and held her door open for her. In the elevator he scanned his fingerprint. Hers was in the system now too. She could ride up and down to the penthouse using her own thumb.

Jackson hurried to the door and pressed his palm to the sensor. She now had access to that, too, but it was nice that he was being chivalrous. He held the door open for her as she stepped inside.

The apartment was just as she remembered it. Clean white lines and modern design. She loved the warm light coming in through the windows and the way she could see everything from up here. The two floors, as well as the wrap-around windows really did make a difference to the view.

She stepped inside and found herself looking at one of the pieces of art hanging on the wall. It was a huge canvas print of snowy mountains. Just looking at them made her feel invigorated.

"You like it?" Jackson asked, coming up beside her.

"I do," she replied. "Do you know where these mountains are?"

Jackson grinned. "The Alps. I know, because I took the photo."

"Really?" Emma turned impressed.

Jackson nodded. "I am a man of many talents."

"I would love to see mountains someday. They look amazing."

Jackson frowned. "You've never seen the mountains?"

She shook her head. "I was born and raised here in the city. My parents didn't have much money for us to travel. Mountains are on my bucket list of things to see."

He looked at her like she had two heads for a moment before motioning down a hallway. "This way."

They walked through a gourmet kitchen where Emma could see a wine fridge as well as every kitchen gadget she'd ever heard of. She didn't linger long as she didn't want to lose sight of Jackson. The apartment was as big as many houses.

They went to the master bedroom. A giant bed dominated the middle of the room with soft gray furniture on the sides. It reminded Emma of a spa she'd once been to. Everything was warm, soft, and comfortable.

Jackson made sure she was still with him as he went to the master closet. He opened the door and she did her best not to gasp.

The closet was bigger than her bedroom.

"This side is yours," Jackson explained, motioning to a series of empty shelves. She could fit her entire wardrobe and then some in the space he had just given her.

"This is a bit more than a drawer," Emma said, taking a step inside. Her small bag of things felt pitiful now. She should have brought the sweater.

"I want you to be comfortable," he replied with a shrug.

"Where did you put your things?" she asked. Opposite her shelves were matching ones, only filled with dark leather shoes, suits and various other clothing.

"It was all last season." Her eyes got big and he laughed. "I didn't really have much there. All I need are suits for work, gym stuff, and a couple of things to wear to the beach. It wasn't hard to condense."

"Thank you," she whispered, looking back at her new closet space.

"Of course," he replied. He checked his watch. "I'm afraid I have to get to work. Will you be alright by yourself?"

"Yes," she assured him. Then she stopped and gave him a naughty grin. "What if I said I wouldn't be?"

"Then I would cancel my very important meeting with my VP of design and stay with you." He narrowed his eyes. "You aren't going to make me stay, are you? It really is kind of important."

"No, I won't," she promised with a laugh. "I'll save it for when I really need you to stay with me."

He grinned at her. "I'll be home in three hours. Any preference for dinner?"

"Your pick," she said. "I don't know what your kitchen looks like or where the nearest grocery store is."

"You don't have to cook. Unless you want to. There's a menu hanging in a binder on the fridge. Look through it. The chef will make it for us."

"The chef?" Emma asked.

"Yes, the chef. I don't have time to make my own healthy meals every night," he told her. "So pick something, and we'll have dinner tonight. Here."

She loved the way he looked at her. Like dinner at home with her was something worth looking forward to.

"Okay." Her stomach did the happy flutter again. "I'll see you then. You should get going or you'll be late."

"Maybe I just don't want to leave," he said softly. Her heart trembled.

"I don't really want you to either," she whispered back.

"But, you did say it was important. And, I'll make it worth your while after dinner."

His eyes lit up. "That sounds like a perfect idea."

He leaned over and kissed the top of her head. She warmed from the touch of his lips straight down to her toes.

"Have fun unpacking," he said, and then quickly turned and headed out the door before he could change his mind.

Emma watched him go, her heart beating fast. Unpacking was nice, and she was looking forward to a delicious meal, but it was the after-dinner activity that she was most excited about...

 *mma*

Emma fiddled with the strings on her satin robe, waiting for Jackson to come home that night. He was due home any minute now and she was counting the seconds.

She lay on the white leather couch under the light of the lamp. She knew that she would be the first thing he would see when he walked in the door, because she'd checked it to make sure. She'd stood in the entryway and made sure that the light hit only the couch. She just hoped that it looked as sexy in real life as it did her mind.

She stretched her legs out along the cool leather, feeling the satin of her robe slip slightly. It was the only thing she had on. Just a pale pink satin robe tied at her waist. She could already imagine Jackson's fingers touching her through the soft fabric and she shivered.

She hoped he came home soon.

Steps in the hallway drew her attention. She held her

breath as she heard someone place their hand to the door and the soft click of the lock as it released.

What if it wasn't him? she suddenly thought. What if this wasn't Jackson, but one of the cleaning staff or an assistant? They were about to walk in on Emma in a rather compromising position. Emma held her breath as the door opened. If it wasn't Jackson, it was too late to do anything about it now.

The door swung open and Jackson stepped inside. Emma let out a small breath, glad that it was him and not an overbearing assistant. She could just image his secretary or Jane walking in.

He shrugged out of his dark suit jacket, not yet noticing her on the couch. His shoulders slumped and he moved slowly as he kicked off his shoes. It must have been a hard day at work.

She cleared her throat, making him look up. He paused and his mouth dropped as he took her in. She lay in the lamplight, all soft curves and sex. She'd purposefully curled her hair into soft waves and experimented with eye makeup until she had just the right bedroom eyes.

"Welcome home, Jackson," she purred, making sure to keep her voice low and seductive.

A slow smile crossed his face and his shoulders came back up. The cocky walk that she loved was back as he moved through the apartment to stand before her. His eyes went up and down her body, taking in every inch.

"I could get used to this," he murmured, still looking her over like he didn't believe she was real. His eyes finally met hers and she could see the lust shining through.

"I was wondering when you were going to get home." Her hand went to the silky collar of her robe and she tugged on it gently to reveal just a hint of smooth skin underneath. She liked that he swallowed hard and stared.

"Work went long," he said, his eyes still glued to the bare skin of her chest. She let the robe open just a little more. "If I had known this was waiting for me, I would have been home hours ago."

She grinned and stood from the couch She flipped off the light, letting just the pale glow from the city lights fill the room. With a grin, she undid the ties to the robe and let the fabric slide to the floor. The pale silk pooled around her ankles as she stood naked before him in the pale twilight. She knew the lack of light would hide her flaws.

His reaction made all the waiting worth it. His eyes dilated, his mouth opened, and she could see the growing bulge in his pants. She rather liked having this effect on him. She knew that he found her beautiful. She knew that he found her sexually attractive, but to see his actual reaction would never get old.

She felt like a goddess when he looked at her like that.

He reached out a finger and caressed the arch of her collarbone, his finger then tracing the curve of her shoulder down her arm. Goosebumps popped out along her skin, but it wasn't from cold. It was pure desire at being touched. His fingers caught the swell of her breast, skimming along the curve and barely touching her.

Her nipples hardened in front of his eyes. Hunger blossomed on his face as he cupped her breast in his warm hand, his thumb rubbing against the hard nipple. Jackson's pupils nearly took over the green of his eyes.

She took a step forward, threading her hand over his shoulder and into his hair as she pressed her naked body against his suit. She could feel the warm, hard spot at her groin as she leaned in, drawing his lips to hers.

He tasted so good. Every time he kissed her he tasted better. His mouth opened and his tongue quested into her waiting mouth, tangling with her tongue. His hand was still on her breast, playing with the nipple while the other hand went to her hip and pulled her further into him.

She pulled back, gazing up at him through long lashes and grinning. She rocked her naked hips into his, feeling him harden further. With the hand not around his neck, she grabbed his tie, fisting the silk, and pulled him in for another kiss.

This kiss was urgent. She wanted to feel him inside of her. She wanted his hard length to fill her. Heat was building in her core and he was the only one who could put it out.

He kissed her, letting her be in control for a moment. She smiled as she kissed him, enjoying the idea that the naked woman was the one in control of the clothed, powerful businessman.

He groaned, and his hand tightened on her hip. She wasn't in quite as much control as he let her think. He was bigger and stronger. His hip thrust into her, letting her know that he was going to fuck her the moment he had the chance.

And she was very okay with that.

She relaxed her hold on his tie, letting the crumpled silk go. She grinned at him. This wasn't all she had planned. She looked up into those green eyes that she adored and slowly went to her knees before him.

She loved the way his muscles clenched as she reached for his belt. He was forcing himself to hold still for her so she could undo his belt and pants button. They came away easily enough and she tugged them down. He kicked them free.

The bulge in his briefs was monstrous. She had a hard time believing that this thing fit inside of her, yet looking at it she wanted it there. She wanted to feel him stretch her out, filling her to completion.

She looked up at him, watching his face twist with desire as she pulled the briefs down, freeing his monster.

Hard, long, and thick right before her eyes. She licked her

lips, ready to taste him. She licked him from balls to tip like he was an ice cream cone about to drip. The groan that came from deep within him made her go wet. She pressed her knees together, wanting to focus on his pleasure before her own.

Slowly, making eye contact the entire time, she rose up slightly, opening her mouth. She brought the tip of her cock to her lips, loving the way his mouth twisted with desire, his eyes begging her to take him inside of her.

With a grin of her own, she brought her hot mouth over his hard cock. He whimpered softly, his hands going to tangle in her hair and pleasure painting his face. She used her tongue to press up on the sensitive flesh, her mouth sucking and licking.

He was delicious. She loved the way she could feel his pulse pound through his cock when he was in her mouth. He grew harder than she thought possible as she used her mouth to tease and tempt him. She wondered if she could get him to come like this, spilling his seed into her mouth.

The idea turned her on and she sucked harder.

He groaned with pleasure, his hands tightening in her hair. His hips started to thrust into her mouth, filling her to almost gagging. She slid one hand down her naked body, placing it between her legs and searching for her clit. It was too good not to at least give herself a little bit of pleasure.

She felt his as clench and his jaw tightened as he looked down on her.

"That's so hot," he whispered, watching her pleasure both him and herself at the same time. He thrust deeper into her mouth, and she wondered just how long he had left before he exploded.

With a growl he pulled on her hair, forcing her to stand before him. His eyes were wild with lust as he made her stand.

"Turn around," he commanded. She did as she was told. He gave her a gentle push on the shoulder, guiding her onto the couch. Her hands rested on the back while her knees went to the seat.

She grinned, and stuck out her ass, waving it slightly before him. He wasn't going to come in her mouth, and that was okay with her as long as he came deep inside her. She was getting him one way or another.

He took his throbbing cock in his hand and guided himself into her opening. She gasped with pleasure as he slid in on her spit, the blow job making things smoother for both of them. He thrust deep, plunging his entire length all the way inside of her.

She felt skewered in the most erotic way. He was so big that he filled her to breaking, and she cried out as he did it again.

He was in control now. One hand went to her hip, and the other grabbed her long hair. She arched her back and he hissed with pleasure as he slammed into her once again. He tugged on her hair, forcing her head to go back and thus her back to arch. The arch moved her ass into the air.

He smacked her ass, making her cry out with pleasure. It didn't hurt, but instead brought even more sensation to her. Plus, it told her that he was in control. He was dominant, and taking what he wanted from her.

He wanted her body.

He pounded into her, going so deep she was sure he would break her, but causing so much pleasure with every thrust that she didn't care. Her body cried out for release, aching with such heat and need that she wasn't sure she could contain it.

He must have felt her tighten because his thrusts intensified. It was too much. She fell over the edge of pleasure, losing herself to his cock in her body. Electric bliss radiated out from her core, squeezing and tingling every fiber of her being.

She felt him explode just as her orgasm began to ebb. He shouted, plunging deep into her body, forcing himself into her tightness and causing another orgasm to rip through her. This time, they were both lost to pleasure, the rhythmic clenching and release spurring the other into more pleasure.

She could feel his seed fill her and complete her in a primal way. The hot power of it raced through her system. The power of life filled her with white desire.

For a moment, Emma forgot how to breathe. She forgot everything that wasn't Jackson buried inside of her and the pleasure only he could give her. She felt rather than heard her mouth scream his name.

Together, they collapsed into the cool leather of the couch. His body was hot and sticky behind her, both of them coated in sweat. Her body ached in the best possible way.

"And here I thought we were having dinner," Jackson mumbled, still buried inside of her. His voice was low and throaty.

"Dessert first tonight," she told him. He pushed a little deeper, still hard inside of her, and she moaned.

"I think I can get used to this," he whispered.

"Me too," she agreed. "Me too."

Grace waved from a small table, motioning Emma to come sit with her. Emma smiled politely at the restaurant hostess and hurried over to see her friend.

"Sorry I'm late," Emma apologized. "I forget how long it takes to get anywhere downtown."

"Well, that's because you're living in the center of the city," Grace replied. She winked at her friend. "Although, honestly, if I were you, I'd probably never leave the building."

Emma chuckled. If she never left the building, it was because she was too busy being naked with Jackson. His nice big bed with the wide windows was perfect for lazy mornings, afternoons, evenings and nights. She was surprised she was still able to walk in a straight line after all of the time spent in bed.

"I ordered us coffee," Grace said. She set the menu down and smiled at her friend. "Now, you have to tell me about dating Jackson Weathers. You never even told me you knew him!"

Emma shrugged. "You know that he owns the building with the Coffee Shack I used to work in, right?"

Grace nodded. "And what? You served him coffee and he fell in love with how you do a triple pour?"

Emma chuckled. "Basically. We'd talked on and off for a long time, but I never thought he was interested. The man is known for dating movie stars and ballerinas. I'm not exactly his usual type."

"So what happened? What changed his mind?" Grace asked. "Not that I need to catch a new man. I'm just curious."

"He's tired of ballerinas and movie stars," Emma explained. She and Jackson had come up with the official story of how they started dating. "He'd wanted to ask me out for months, but after he got burned by another starlet, he finally just did it."

"And?" Grace tucked her hands under her chin. "Love at first sight?"

"We'd met before, remember?" Emma chuckled. "But, yeah. He took me out on a date and we talked for hours. It's strange, but we actually have a lot in common."

"It's so romantic," Grace replied. "It's a good thing you didn't apply to that want-ad you were telling me about. The one to marry the Canadian business man? Jackson Weathers is a huge step up."

"That's one way of looking at it." Emma quickly took a sip of her water and then changed the subject. "Where's my little man? I thought you were bringing Sammy today."

Grace shook her head. "I was, but he's got a fever. So does Chris. The two of them are staying home watching cartoons and taking it easy. I'm staying out of the house as much as possible in the hopes I don't catch it too. I'm under strict orders to bring home soup and to stay healthy. Now, I want to hear what it's like to live with a billionaire."

"It's like staying in a fancy hotel all the time. We have a butler, a concierge, a chef, cleaning crews, and a personal trainer down in the private gym," Emma told her. "It's so different than before. I don't have to do any chores. I'm eating great and working out. I totally see how celebrities can have the amazing bodies they do. It's possible when it's the only thing you have to worry about."

"It sounds heavenly," Grace told her. She paused. "You're still going to watch Sammy for us every once in a while, though? He loves you."

"Of course I'll watch Sammy," Emma assured her. "Nothing's changed."

"Okay," Grace said, sounding relieved. "I just don't know what we'd do without you. I don't want you getting all fancy and forgetting about us."

"Never," Emma promised.

The waitress came to take their order and the conversation moved to Emma describing how seasick she had gotten sailing, and how sweet and normal Jackson was. She wanted Grace to know that Jackson wasn't some immortal god summoned from on high. He was just a normal man, even if he was a god in the sack.

The two enjoyed breakfast before Grace got a call that Sammy needed her. Grace gave Emma a hug.

"Okay, make sure you call me this week," Grace reminded her with an extra long hug. "Your mom would be so happy for you."

The comment nearly knocked Emma over. "What?"

"Do you remember when we were kids? We'd play dress-up and you always wanted to be the knight instead of the princess," Grace said, her eyes going distant as she went back in time. "Your mom always said that was good, that you should be your own hero. You didn't want anything to do with princes. She said that you should fall in love with the man and not because he was the knight in shining armor. Love matters, not who is the prince."

As Grace said the words, Emma could hear her mother's voice. The soft scent of freshly washed linen that her mother always smelled like hit her hard.

Emma's throat tightened.

"And now, you picked a prince because he likes you, not because he's a prince. Your mom would be happy for you," she repeated.

Shame hit Emma square in the stomach and she felt like she might throw up. But, she had to keep up the appearance. It was critical that she maintain that she and Jackson were in love and that's why they were dating.

"Thank you, Grace," Emma whispered, struggling to keep herself under control. "I'll see you soon."

Grace gave her one more hug before hurrying off to care for her young son. Emma stared after her, her heart aching in her chest. She quickly left the restaurant, her thoughts flying in all directions.

Emma didn't go home. She didn't go up to Jackson's and she didn't go to her new place. Instead, she went to the cemetery to see her mom and dad. For the first time since signing the contract, she was starting to regret her decision.

The cemetery was peaceful and quiet. Big, tall oak tress dotted the edges and the white tombstones stood at attention as she walked in. Guilt pulled at her feet as she made her way along the paths to where her parents rested. She hadn't come in far too long.

"Hi, Mom. Hi, Dad." Emma stood before two gravestones.

They were simple and small, but they were a mark on the world that her parents had been here.

She sat down on the green grass between them and sighed.

"So, it's been a while, and I'm sorry about that," she started. She took a deep breath. "I need to know that you're okay with this. I'm going to marry him. I'm going to have his baby. I know it's a terrible plan, especially given his reputation, but I agreed to it."

Her parents said nothing.

"What I'm really worried about is that I'm developing feelings for him." Emma's throat tightened. "I really, really like him. Possibly even love him, though it's been so fast and it's not part of the deal. What if he humiliates me? What if he doesn't love me back? What if he leaves me and I have to watch him break my heart because it's in the contract?"

Tears trickled down Emma's face. She didn't know what her mother would say here. Her mother had died when she was ten. It was old enough to have wonderful memories, but young enough to have missed out on all the parts of growing past childhood.

She never had a discussion with her mother about boys, other than to say that Bobby Neelson had cooties. Jackson probably had cooties too, but it was a different kind of conversation.

Emma looked over at her dad's tombstone. After Mom died, he'd shut down. He had made sure that Emma had the physical necessities and did well in school, but his heart was gone. He'd died of a heart attack her sophomore year of college.

If he had anything to say, it would be to have safe sex. Which she wasn't, and that was kind of the point and the problem.

"I could use a sign," she whispered. She wasn't sure what

her parents would think of this. She was sure if they knew the whole story that they wouldn't approve. But what about the story they told the public? Would her mom be pleased she was marrying a billionaire? That Emma had chosen a prince after all?

She sighed and waited. The wind ruffled the grass, but there was no wise answer. Her mother's ghost didn't appear and tell her that everything was going to be okay. There was no message from beyond the grave that she was doing the right thing or that she should run away as fast as possible.

It made Emma's heart hurt that much more.

She was alone with this decision.

mma

She'd stayed at the cemetery for hours waiting for a sign that had never come. She had cried, but didn't feel better. She just felt empty.

Jackson's apartment was empty when Emma got home. The summer sun cast long shadows as it slowly moved toward evening. The world glowed with orange light, yet Emma didn't see it. Her thoughts were elsewhere.

What if in a few months he didn't want her anymore? Had she really thought this through?

Granted, she'd still have money, but she was starting to develop feelings for him. She liked the way he smiled at her. What if he didn't feel the same? What if those emotions were one sided? What if after they had a child, he went back to his old philandering ways?

It would break her heart and destroy her.

She was starting to worry that she'd made a mistake. This

had started out being about money and comfort, but now it was turning into feelings. That certainly wasn't part of the bargain.

She sighed and flopped onto the couch in the main room. She'd gone to Jackson's apartment rather than her own. She wasn't entirely sure why, but it felt more comfortable here.

"You just need to get settled in," she told herself. She ignored the fact that the movers had already unpacked everything, including the two boxes she'd had left over from her previous move.

"Is that you, Emma?" Jackson called out, surprising her. She thought he was still at work.

"Yeah, it's me," she said, sitting up straight on the couch. She wiped at her eyes, realizing that she probably looked like she'd been crying all afternoon. That was not how she wanted Jackson to see her.

"You're home early," he said, coming into the living room. He wore a comfortable t-shirt and gym shorts, but his hair was wet, indicating he'd showered. He looked handsome as hell. He always looked handsome as hell to her. He looked at her and frowned. "Everything okay?"

"Yeah, everything's fine," she told him. She did her best to smile, but she knew it didn't touch her eyes.

"I don't believe you," he replied. His green eyes went dark as he looked her over. He sat on the floor in front of her, taking her hands in his. "What's wrong, Emma? You can tell me."

"It's nothing." She pulled her hands back into her lap and immediately felt guilty for doing so.

"No, it's not. Something has you upset," Jackson said. "You tell me who needs murdered and it's done. I know people in the mafia."

That elicited a smile from her.

"Tell me," he said. His eyes were gentle as he reached for her hands again. "Tell me so I can fix it."

"I went and saw my parents today." Emma's voice quavered and she couldn't look him in the face. "I don't know what they'd say if they knew what we were doing."

Jackson sighed and nodded his head.

"I just... I don't know..." Emma started to cry. She didn't want to. She didn't mean to cry, but the tears just poured out of her. She'd thought she'd gotten all the tears out at the cemetery, but yet here was a fresh batch.

Jackson moved from the floor to the couch, putting his arm around her shoulder and pulling her into him. He comforted her, rubbing her back and rocking gently as she released the flood of tears. It felt better when he held her.

"It's okay," he whispered.

"No, it's not," Emma shot back. "I agreed to this. It's a good plan. I'm going to get what I want, and so are you. I don't know why I'm upset."

Jackson smoothed a dark hair off her tear-stained cheek. He was gentle and kind with every motion.

"I want you to be happy, Emma," he said slowly. "I want us both to be happy. And I am."

"You are?" she asked, sniffling at the end.

He smiled softly and nodded. "I am. I think we're a good match. And I think that your parents would be proud of how well you get along with people. How happy you can make anyone. Even me."

She sniffled again, but the tears were starting to dry up. He caressed her face with his finger.

"Can I show you how happy I am that you're doing this with me?" he asked. "That I have the same fears as you, but that when I'm with you, they go away?"

She looked up, seeing only the beautiful light in his green eyes. Even if he didn't love her the way the prince did in the storybooks, he wasn't going to hurt her. She knew what she was in for. He'd never lied to her.

She needed to stop worrying and just live in the now. Live in the moment where they were. In this moment, there was no worry. There was no judgment.

Just them.

"Okay," she whispered.

He smiled at her, and her worries began to fade. They were still there, in the back of her mind, but when he looked at her like that, they weren't a problem anymore. They were on par with trying to remember if she turned out the bathroom light the night before. It was something to worry about, but not really.

Jackson scooped her up in his arms and carried her into the bedroom. She clung to him. He would take her pain away. He would show her that everything was alright. When he was with her, she forgot everything but the pleasure he showed her.

It didn't matter what anyone else thought, she realized. It only mattered what she thought. What Jackson thought. If this was enough for them, then there was no one to judge them.

She was happy with him. She loved him.

She pushed her fear of the future aside. There was only the now. She would love him. She would take the risk that one day he would look at someone else. It would kill her, but the way she felt towards him right now was worth it.

He was worth the risk. Their relationship was worth the risk.

She reached up and kissed him.

She was his.

It was supposed to be their first real public appearance as a couple and Jackson was nervous. He wasn't nervous about Emma, but rather how the public would react to her. She was so sweet and warm, he knew they would love her if they gave her a chance.

He was worried that they wouldn't give her that chance. He knew how cruel the media could be. He knew that they could rip her to shreds. That was the last thing in the world that he wanted.

Jackson pushed his fears aside and waited patiently for Emma to emerge from the bathroom. The hair and makeup ladies had both left, so she just needed to put on her dress. It was another of Thad's design choices, so he knew she was going to look stunning.

The bathroom door opened and she stepped out. Jackson's use of the word stunning wasn't enough to describe her. She was radiant. Gorgeous. Breathtaking.

Scratch all of those, he thought to himself. *There isn't a word for how beautiful she looks.*

"What do you think?" Emma asked, her voice unsure as she held out her arms for his approval. Jackson didn't know much about dress design, but this one fit her to a tee. Her dress was black with just a hint of shine to it. White cutout patterns accented her waist and bust, giving her the illusion of a corseted waist. Her hair hung around her shoulders in soft waves.

He wanted to run his fingers through those waves. He wanted to hike up her dress and take her right there, to be honest. He felt himself harden at the thought of bending her over and how the dress would ride up her ass...

"Jackson?" Emma's nervous voice broke through his thoughts.

"You look perfect," he told her, keeping his desire to hike up her dress quiet.

"I just want to make sure that I'm doing what you need me to do." She chewed on a delicious red lip for a moment before realizing what she was doing.

He loved that she was putting her whole heart into making this work. It was more than he expected.

His watch vibrated notifying him that the car was ready to take them. He tapped the notification and smiled at Emma.

"Are you ready?"

She took a deep breath and nodded. He offered her his arm, making her smile, and together they walked to the car.

Emma said little on the drive to the party. Jackson had been invited to a high profile charity fundraiser and felt that this was the perfect opportunity to present the two of them as a couple. His PR adviser, Jane, agreed.

There would be lots of photographers and press. Jane had drooled imagining the red carpet photo of the two of the walking hand in hand. It would go viral. He'd warned Emma that she would be on the cover of every tabloid magazine tomorrow.

"Why will I be on the cover?" she asked, as the limo turned toward the gala. "You have a new hot date every other week. Why is this different?"

Jackson shifted slightly in his seat. "Because I am going to be the attentive boyfriend tonight," he explained. "Also, I never bring dates to these things. I always pick someone up there."

Emma's eyes widened. "So, I'm your first real date?"

"I've been on plenty of real dates," he replied, only a little defensively.

That made her smile wider. "I'm your first real date," she repeated. "You *like* me."

"I'm supposed to marry you, remember?"

"You like me and I'm your first real date," she repeated in a sing-song tone. She sat up a little straighter and grinned at him. "You're gonna marry me."

"Not if you keep that up," he teased her. She kept grinning at him, knowing that he was playing. "You still clear on what we need to do tonight?"

She put on a serious face. "I'm supposed to tell everyone how wonderful and loving you are. That we met at the coffee shop and you asked me out. Then we talked for hours and are madly in love."

"Good. What else?"

"That I've seen a change in you. I've served you coffee for over a year, and thus I am qualified to say that you are so much more than a playboy exterior. You have seen the error of your ways and are turning over a new leaf because I am so very, very awesome."

She grinned at him and winked. The last part was extra.

"I'm glad you feel confident," he said as the limo came to a stop. He turned and watched her swallow hard. She was nervous and trying her best not to show it.

"I'm ready," she said, squaring her shoulders. She flashed him a grin. "I won't let you down. By the end of the night, everyone will think we are madly in love and that I have tamed your bad boy ways."

He kissed her cheek, careful not to smear her delicate makeup.

"You're going to do great."

The door opened and he helped her out of the limo. She did her best to keep a smooth smile on her face, but he could see her eyes darting everywhere to take everything in.

He looked around, seeing the event through new eyes.

The red carpet, the photographers, the beautiful people, and the obvious display of wealth suddenly became very apparent to him. He'd become so used to it that this felt normal, but he could only imagine what Emma felt. It must be overwhelming.

She clung to him like she was holding onto a life preserver in a stormy sea. Her smile was bright, but her hands trembled against his arm as she made sure he couldn't leave her side. He was half afraid he might find bruises on his arms from her grip.

"You're doing great," he coached as they entered the main area. There were less photographers here and more guests, so he hoped she could relax a little and enjoy the party.

For the first time, he was worried about someone else having a good time. It was strange to think that he had her coming home with him either way, but that he wanted her to be happy.

He usually only wanted his date to have fun so they'd come home with him.

He steered her towards a friendly face.

"Emma, I'd like you to meet a friend of mine," he introduced her. "This is Ed Hallen. He's my vice president of operations."

Ed wasn't in on the secret about Emma. No one but Jane and his secretary knew the truth. They were the only people he trusted with this, because he paid them enough to stay quiet. His success was their success.

"So you're the one who has Jackson leaving the office early," Ed replied, smiling at them both warmly. "I must say, it's a pleasure to meet you."

"Thank you," she replied. Her grip on Jackson's arm lessened a fraction.

"Don't be scared of the guests here," Ed advised. "They all bark, but none of them bite. If anything, they'll be curious how you managed to keep him this long. I must say I am curious myself."

"Emma is amazing," Jackson replied for her. "She's smart and funny and obviously beautiful. What isn't to love?"

"Love, huh?" Ed didn't look completely convinced, but he shrugged and smiled anyway. "Speaking of love, have you met my wife? She'd love to meet you."

Emma looked over at Jackson, her eyes making sure that she was doing the right thing. Jackson gave her a subtle nod. Ed's wife was a sweetheart who would spread the news of Jackson's change of heart. It was what they came here to do.

"Have fun," Jackson told her. "I need to go schmooze a little."

"And you can't flirt with this lovely lady on your arm," Ed teased. He motioned to a different part of the room. "My wife is over by the bar."

Jackson gave Emma's hand a gentle squeeze as she let go of his arm. He could see her nerves in the small movements she made. Her breath came fast and her eyes were wide. If he didn't know her, he wouldn't know to look.

She flashed him an smile and followed Ed. He watched her walk away, sad to see her go but enjoying the view. With a deep breath of his own, he went to mingle. He needed to show he'd turned over a new leaf and not flirt with the beautiful women of the party.

He should have felt disappointed about not being able to chase the women here. The hot new movie starlet was here and just his type, yet he had no desire to speak with her. If anything, he wanted to go find Emma.

It was a strange sensation. He shook his head. He was just getting into character, he told himself. He was method acting, and just like actors, his character bled onto his real life person. It sounded like a fine theory as to why he had no real desire to seduce the movie star.

The night went slowly. Jackson made sure to talk to as many people as possible, all the time working in how happy Emma made him. He made sure to mention that she'd moved into his building but was actually spending most of her time at his place. He mentioned how wonderful it was to have a roommate.

And it didn't feel like he was lying.

The crowd inside the fundraiser increased. Jackson made sure to keep an eye out for Emma. She was always in the back of his mind and he wanted to make sure she was alright. As much as he had promised her that everything would go well at the party, the crowd here could eat her alive if she stumbled.

Luckily, she was doing amazing.

From his spot in the room, he could see her smiling and laughing with a set of wives. As far as visibility was concerned, she was one of them now. She'd charmed them, just as she had charmed him. And she appeared to do it effortlessly.

He smiled and took a sip of his drink. She was doing so well, he was starting to relax. Maybe this night could go as well as he'd hoped.

That's when he saw Max. Max Singleton was the Public Relations officer for the Innocence Company. Jackson had hired him several years ago, but had found the man to be willing to do anything to get ahead. Jackson hadn't approved of the man's methods and fired him.

Max was a snake and exactly the last person Emma should talk to. He would figure out their little plan in two seconds flat and then announce it to the entire room. Max would ruin everything.

Jackson set down his drink and hurried across the room until someone caught his arm and attempted to pull him into a conversation. Jackson tried to get away, but he was too late.

Max was talking to Emma, and she looked panicked...

mma

"And how exactly did you two meet?" the man asked Emma.

He looked nice enough with his tuxedo and smoothly combed brown hair, but there was something in his ice blue eyes that made her squirm. Something that made her want to run from the man.

"Excuse me, I'm afraid I didn't get your name," she said, doing her best to be polite. She glanced around, looking for Jackson, but she didn't see him anywhere.

"Max," the man replied. He smiled in what she assumed was supposed to be a friendly smile, but it felt more like looking at a shark. "Max Singleton."

"It's very nice to meet you, Max," Emma told him. "Would you excuse me for a moment?"

Emma gave him a short smile and turned to step away. Something told her that if Jackson and her plan were to work, she needed to get away from this man as quickly as possible.

"No, I won't actually," Max replied, catching her arm. "I have far too many questions. Where in the world did Jackson find you? You're perfect."

"Excuse me?" Emma pulled her arm away from him hard enough to hurt.

"You're the perfect fake wife," Max replied. "Cute, bubbly, and you probably want a whole litter of kids. What did Jackson promise you? I hope it wasn't his faithfulness. He's not exactly known for that."

"You have no idea what you're talking about," Emma said, trying to keep her voice calm even though she felt like screaming. This man had seen right through her. "Jackson and I are very much in love."

"You almost sound like you believe it." Max chuckled. He pointed a finger at her. "You're good. You're really good. If I didn't know he needed an image change, I would believe it. You are an amazing actress. Really."

Emma stumbled back from the man. She crashed into another couple, spilling the woman's drink all over her expensive dress. The woman was thin and gorgeous with long, straight, platinum hair and a body that belonged as a centerfold of a swimsuit magazine. The man beside her looked furious at the interruption and Emma felt like crying.

She'd been doing so well up until now. Emma wished she could melt into the floor and disappear.

"Do you know who I am?" the woman shouted at her. "Do you know who designed this dress you just ruined?"

"I am so sorry," Emma apologized. "Please, let me go get some napkins--"

"You think napkins are going to fix this?" The woman scoffed at her. "You obviously don't belong here."

Emma's mouth opened, but she couldn't think of

anything to say. The only upside was that Max had disappeared. Although, he was probably just hiding in the shadows and laughing as she floundered and failed.

"I am so, so, sorry, miss." Emma's face was hot with shame. She couldn't even see the wet spot on the woman's black dress anymore, but that didn't matter. She was failing at her one mission at this party: to get people to like and believe her.

"I can't believe Jackson would bring a nobody like you," the woman sneered.

Emma stood there, helpless.

"Kristy, how nice to see you," Jackson said, magically showing up at Emma's elbow. He took her hand and tucked it into the crook of his arm.

Relief at being saved filled her, followed promptly by shame. This Max fellow knew the truth and now she'd managed to ruin this woman's dress. This was exactly what Jackson didn't need.

"Jackson, did you see what your little *girlfriend* just did to my dress?" The word girlfriend hurled from the woman's mouth like an insult, making Emma wince.

"Kristy, there's nothing there," Jackson replied smoothly. "Much like my desire to speak with you."

Emma's mouth opened a little in shock. Jackson never spoke that way to her. Jackson went to turn and walk away. Emma was all to happy to follow along.

"Jackson, I know that you still want me," Kristy replied, her voice dark and full of seduction. Emma watched as the man who had been standing beside Kristy turned his head and looked surprised.

"No, I don't. Once was more than enough and I never make the same mistake twice," Jackson replied, his voice light and cheerful. He leaned toward the man. "Be careful with this one, friend. She's a tiger in the sack, but she's gone through two rich husbands. You sure you want to be hubby number three?"

"Jackson!" The woman switched tactics, going to angry rather than seductive. Even angry, she was gorgeous.

"Come on Emma, we have better places to be," Jackson replied with a polite smile as if the woman hadn't just shouted at him. He turned, pulling Emma with him, and walked away.

Emma followed, surprised at how calm he appeared even while the woman shouted after him. Jackson pulled Emma to a small room off to the side. It looked like it was the coat storage area during the winter, but since it was summer, there were just boxes of storage and one of the caterers texting on his phone.

"Get out," Jackson told him. The man looked up in surprise and quickly left. Jackson shut the door to the small room behind him.

"I'm so sorry, Jackson," Emma began. Hot tears welled up behind her eyes. "I should have just walked away and, and-"

Jackson wrapped his arms around her. She was sure he was going to yell. She was sure he was going to tell her the contract was done and she could start to pack her things. She was sure of it, yet he was holding her.

"You couldn't have known Kristy was going to scream at you," he said after a moment. "You did fine with her."

A little hope worked into her chest.

"Max on the other hand..." Jackson shook his head.

"I didn't say anything," Emma quickly told him. "I told him we were in love, but... but I don't think he believed me."

He hugged her a little tighter. "It's okay."

"No, it's not," she said, pushing him away. "I was supposed to be convincing tonight and he saw right through me. I don't know who he is, but Max Singleton suspects exactly what we're doing."

Jackson stood silent for a moment, his broad shoulders unmoving. "He's the PR manager for The Innocence Company. If he had tried to solve this problem instead of Jane, I imagine he would have come up with a similar solution."

Emma stared at him, amazed at his calm. She felt like things were spinning wildly out of control. Max knew. Kristy was off telling the entire party how terrible Emma was. And yet, Jackson just stood there. Being calm.

"Why are you not freaking out?" Emma asked. She wanted to pace the floor. She wanted to hit something, throw something to the ground. Nervous energy crackled through her skin.

"What would freaking out accomplish?" Jackson asked with a shrug. "It's two people. Max might be a problem, but he has no proof. And Kristy? She's a joke. Always has been."

"What do you mean?" Emma asked.

"Kristy is a certified gold digger. She's working her way through rich husbands, and her little stunt this evening was because she's mad I'm not next," he explained. "She is jealous of you, so I'd say her little freak-out is actually in our favor. She believes that you have snagged the prize."

He motioned to himself like he was a prize winning fish on display.

"Oh." That made Emma feel a little bit better. "Did you ever sleep with her?"

Jackson looked at her with those green eyes that made her knees weak. "Do you really want the answer to that?"

Emma thought about it. "Not really. It's in the past either way."

Jackson nodded.

"What about Max? What do we do about him?" Emma asked. There she felt like a failure. She should have done more to convince him. She should have done something. Anything.

"We make it so he has no proof," Jackson replied simply. "If everyone else believes it, who cares what he says?"

"So we keep doing what we've been doing," Emma said slowly. She nodded and took a deep breath.

She looked up at Jackson. She had been so sure he was going to be angry, but he had been the exact opposite. He wasn't mad at all that she failed. It felt liberating to know that she didn't have to be perfect all the time to make him happy.

She could fail and he would pick her up.

If that wasn't the foundations for a successful marriage, she wasn't sure what was.

"Kiss me," she ordered him.

He frowned slightly, but did as she asked. A small peck on the lips. She shook her head as he stood up straight. She reached up, wrapping her arm around his neck and pulling his face into hers for a real kiss. One that lit up the room with heat.

All her nervous energy went into the kiss. Her tongue found his, caressing and tasting his lips. She moaned as he wrapped one arm around her hips and the other went to her hair.

She had to pull back. The kiss was too good. If she didn't stop, she was going to rip his clothes off right here in the coat closet. The idea of him naked and pounding her with the party just outside their door was enough to soak her panties through.

Jackson pulled back. "If you kiss me like that, I'm going to take you right here," he told her, his voice low and rough. She could see his excitement building in his pants.

Her fingers itched to undress him.

There was a knock on the door.

"Mr. Weathers? Are you okay in there?" Ed asked through the door.

"We should go back out there," Emma told him.

He just looked at her, his green eyes wild with desire. She could feel him undress her with his eyes and she wanted it. She wanted all of him right then and there.

The knock came again.

Jackson threw open the door. "What?"

"Just making sure everything is alright," Ed replied, trying to peer past Jackson. "Oh, good. I see Emma's with you."

Jackson narrowed his eyes at Ed. "What's that supposed to mean?"

"Nothing, nothing." Ed shook his head. When that didn't stop Jackson from glaring at him, he sighed. "I thought you had something special with Emma. Then you disappeared, and I was worried."

"You were worried I was back to my old tricks?" Jackson asked, a little harshly.

Ed flushed. "Yes."

Jackson motioned to Emma. "You can see I'm not."

"Yes, and I'm glad." Ed gave a nervous wave to Emma. "I'll leave you two alone now."

Jackson slammed the door. "Can you believe that guy?"

Emma smiled and kissed his cheek. It was chaste compared to their most recent kiss.

"Yes, and as you said, it's a good thing."

"A good thing that his first thought was that I was cheating on you?" he asked, his voice rising.

She put her hand on his arm. "Yes. Because he found you with me. He's telling his wife that you're with me. She'll tell the other wives. In a few moments, we'll step out with my hair messed and lipstick smudged and it will only add fuel to the fire that you really are falling for me."

Jackson stared at her and then slowly smiled. "You are really good at this, you know that, right?"

"After we make an appearance, I can show you what else I'm really good at," she promised. She bit her lower lip as she grinned at him.

"Don't tease me," he begged. "I have to at least be able to walk through the room to get out."

She giggled, feeling powerful and desirable. He wanted her. The most powerful man in this building wanted her.

And she wanted him.

"Maybe we should just beeline it for the car," she told him, her own desire creeping up on her. "They can make whatever ideas they want out of that."

Jackson nodded. "They'll talk about your mussed hair and how we just left with smiles on our faces. It's good."

She was breathless with want now. "Definitely good."

He grabbed her hand. "Plus, the limo has a privacy window."

She couldn't breathe she wanted him so bad. She was worried she wouldn't make it all the way to the car before tearing her own dress off and throwing herself at him. From the way he was looking at her, he was thinking the same thing.

Without a word more, Jackson threw open the door and they took off running. Emma giggled as they sprinted through the fancy party, her dress flowing out behind her as they ran for Jackson's limo.

It was the best end she could think of.

mma

Emma barely waited for both of them to get in the limo and the door to close before she kissed him again. She needed his kisses like she needed oxygen. From the way he kissed her back, Jackson felt the same.

The car started moving and Emma decided to utilize the space only a limo could provide.

She pulled up her dress so that she could straddle his waist. He groaned as she moved over him, his hands going to her hips. The soft silky fabric pooled around the two of them as they made out in the back seat of the limo. Jackson nipped at her lower lip, causing her body to heat with desire and she let out a low moan.

"Everything okay back there?" the limo driver asked, glancing back in the mirror.

"Perfect," Jackson replied, his voice tight. She felt his right hand leave her waist and fumble with the buttons until the privacy screen went up.

Emma grinned and glanced around at the darkened windows and privacy screen. "I've never done it in a limo," she remarked.

"Mmm," Jackson mumbled, pressing his face into her cleavage. He tugged on a shoulder strap, causing her dress to fall to the side. He pulled just a little bit more, looking up at Emma and grinning as her breast came free.

"I'm guessing you have," she said, her voice coming out dark and husky. He moved his mouth to her nipple, sucking in the tight nub and making her gasp.

He nibbled and sucked, sending alternating waves of pleasure and desire straight down her spine. She was glad she was able to wear panties with this dress, because she was soaking through them with what he was doing to her.

She arched her back, giving him better access and reveled in the low, male sound of appreciation that came from him. She could feel him growing beneath her, his cock begging to be set free from his pants. Without thinking, she rocked against him, wanting the same thing.

"Fuck," he groaned, the word whispering against the bare skin of her breast. His hands tightened on her hips, not stopping the motion, but instead making sure she kept going.

The car came to a stop.

"Sir, we're here," the driver's voice came over the intercom.

"The one time there's no traffic," Emma whispered. She was fully ready to continue in the limo. The idea of stopping was the last thing she wanted.

Jackson looked up at her. "We get more time if we go upstairs," he told her.

She stuck out her lower lip and rocked against him. "I don't want to wait."

"I'll make it worth your while," he promised. He leaned over and gave her nipple one last tantalizing suck before sliding her sleeve back up her arm.

"You better," she told him, adding a smile to show she wasn't really upset. "And, just so you know, you better do me in the back seat of a limo one day."

He chuckled. "With pleasure," he told her.

She slid off his lap, pulling her dress back down from around her waist. She could see the damp spot on his pants where she'd been grinding against him. He winked at her and opened the limo door up and helped her step out.

Jackson grabbed her hand and dragged her to the elevator. The silver doors opened and he pulled her inside, pushing her against the side wall.

His tongue traced the curve of her neck while one hand went to her breast through the soft fabric of her dress. With his free hand, he hit the authentication button to allow them access to their floor.

The elevator started to rise, just like her temperature. His mouth sucked and licked at the sensitive skin of her throat and shoulders and his hands teased her nipples through the satin of her dress. All the while, he kept her pinned to the elevator wall, keeping her exactly where he wanted her.

Not that she wanted to escape. She wanted to be right there, but there was something about being put in her place that made the deeper parts of her brain light up with desire. It was primal. She half expected him to throw her over his shoulder and carry her into the apartment.

Luckily, no other residents got on the elevator. Emma was glad, because she wouldn't be able to keep her hands off of him. Not when she was this turned on. She didn't want to have to appear proper and polite.

They both nearly missed the soft ding as they arrived on their floor. It was only the change in light that caught Emma's attention that they could leave. She cleared her throat and gave him a gentle push. Jackson didn't move at first, instead licking his lips and pressing her harder against the wall.

The door chimed again before he pulled back. There was a dark fierce desire in his green eyes that heated her straight to the core. He wanted her. He wanted her in the most primal fashion she could imagine. It was only through sheer will power that he was holding onto himself and not taking her completely right there in the elevator.

He grabbed her hand and together they stumbled into his apartment.

As soon as they crossed the threshold into the kitchen, she pushed her body onto his, finding his mouth with hers, and kissed him. She could feel his muscles through his shirt and marveled at the contained strength. He kissed her again as he had before: tough tugs on her lips, a playful tongue. His hands found her face, holding her carefully and tilting her chin up, opening her wider for the kiss.

She melted into him. Her whole body quivered with need that only he could give her. She needed him. His seed, his body, his soul. That was the only thing that could quench the flames growing steadily inside of her.

He drew her to the bedroom, never stopping his kisses, pulling at her straps and zippers until the dress fell away in the hallway. She left it there, a puddle of black and white satin. She stepped into the bedroom first, leaving him in the hallway.

The room was dark. All she had left on was the teeny tiny thong. It was already soaked through with her desire. She turned, watching as he walked through the doorway, the light behind him. Everything was shadows as she stepped back, biting her lip and waiting for him.

Jackson stepped inside, not bothering to close the door,

and turned on the light. Instinctively, she covered herself. Standing seductively in the shadows was one thing, but standing seductively under full light was quite another.

Jackson had slept with super models and ballerinas. She was neither of those things. She had curves and some pounds in places that she wasn't proud of. As much as she wanted him, she wasn't ready to show herself to him completely. Just because there was a contract didn't mean he had to see her with the lights on.

"I want to see you," Jackson said, still standing in the doorway. He came back to her, and gently took her arms from around her body, exposing her to the light and looking down at her round breasts. He ran his fingers up and down the sides of her arms. "I want to see this incredible little body."

She felt her pussy throb at his appraising stare. It made her wet to know he took so much pleasure just looking at her, that he found her curves and smoothness pleasing.

He leaned down and kissed her again, urgent and powerful with his tongue and lips, his jaw pushing and guiding the kiss, up and down, deeper, and then shallow. His hands ran down her arms, cupping her breasts.

He turned her gently so that she was facing the bed, tucking her hair to the side so he could kiss the back of her neck. He kissed down her shoulder, his hands tracing symmetrical paths his kisses followed. She shivered at his touch, wanted him to grab her firmly, but he didn't.

His hands slid onto her back and around to touch her tummy, hugging her against his hard body. She could feel his cock pressing her through his slacks. She wanted to feel it, wanted to feel him. She ground her ass against it.

"Do you have any idea how badly I want you?" he whispered. His breath against her skin made her shiver, and it wasn't with cold. He pressed his solid erection into her ass, letting her feel just how hard he was under his pants.

He kissed her neck and the top of her shoulder, nibbling, his hands sliding around her to hug her hips. His fingers hooked the waistband of the thong. He kissed down her back, over her shoulders and down her spine as he lowered himself, pulling her thong down as he went. He let it roll up as he pulled it over the curve of her tight ass cheeks, then down her bare legs. She could smell her own musk, knew that she had never been this wet with a boy before, so aroused.

He got onto his knees as the thong hit the floor. He touched her ankle so she would step out of it. She did so, but instead of moving away, he slid his hand up to her waist without rising.

"What is it?" she asked, turning around to see what he was doing, but his hands gripped her by the waist firmly to keep her from turning around.

He was staring at her ass, looking up and down the backs of her thighs. His thumbs pressed under the curve of each of her cheeks, squeezing her ass more tightly. He shook them gently, then released his grip, watching them quiver.

"You are amazing," he said. "You know that? Absolutely... amazing."

"Thanks?"

He laughed again, standing up and turning her around. He gave her a rushed kiss, then leaned into her, forcing her to climb on to the bed. She slid up the covers, facing him as he crawled on after her, pursuing her. She put her knees together, her thighs mostly hiding her pussy. She still felt embarrassed in the light, spread like this in front of him. He put one of his thick hands between her knees and parted them.

"No, no," he said, his green eyes bright. "Let me see you."

She let him part her legs. He used both of his hands, lifting each leg outward, dragging her down toward him so she lay flat on her back.

His hands ran down her inner thighs, making her muscles clench and her pussy tingle.

"So pretty," he whispered, dragging a single finger across her entrance. "So wet."

She felt his lips kiss the inside of her knee, then nibble the sensitive flesh of her thigh. Both of his hands rubbing her smooth legs gently as he kissed his way up, up, until he was beside her heat. She was throbbing and tingling. She had never been touched like this. She didn't know her body could feel like this.

His hands parted and held both of her legs just under the curve of her ass cheeks, lifting them under the thighs so that her knees pointed at the ceiling, her calves and her tiny feet bumping on the back of his shoulders. She looked down when she felt his hot breath on her pussy lips. He was staring up at her. He licked his lips.

He pressed his lips against her, the kisses light, making her clench her stomach with each feathery contact, making her feel hot enough to burn through the bed. Then his tongue slid between her smooth lips, pressed in, slid up, moving her juices around, tasting them, until he found the hood of her clit. He salivated heavily on it, running his tongue up and down the side of it, letting his jaw settle against the lips, now puffy in anticipation.

The combination of his touches and licks made her want to squirm in pleasure. The heat spread through her body, her heart began to beat freely, loud in her ears. She curled her toes against the tingling sensations that ran through her.

"Does that feel good?" he asked, his low voice vibrating through her.

"Oh God... yes..."

She felt him rub two of his fingers against her, soaking them in her juices. He pressed his mouth around her clit and sucked on it gently. Heat flashed through her hips, she throbbed as his tongue circled her, slowly. The fingers slid into her easily, but not too deep, toying with her.

"Like this?" he asked.

"Yes... yes," she said, gasping at the combination of sensations, his mouth and tongue, his fingers. He began to rub her more aggressively, as if he were searching for something inside of her.

Then he found it. Her entire body began to tingle, her legs twitched. He slowed his tongue so that it rubbed her clit in hard, slow circles, the sensation so much better when he was slow.

"Lick my pussy slow, like that," she said, gasping.

His fingers dug harder, rubbing, and he started to thrust them in and out, toying with that hot button of nerves inside of her. The feeling that filled her chest was similar to when someone surprised her, scared her—full, bright tension that radiated through her at light speed. Only this built slowly, felt a hundred times more powerful, a tension that gripped her, swirled around like a tornado inside of her, twisting together the sensations of his mouth and tongue.

"Jackson..." she whimpered, taken out of herself, her entire body filled with light and electricity that centered around that hot and urgent pressure between her legs.

He must have sensed it in her. His fingers began to thrust into her roughly. His lips locked around her clit and sucked. In a quick crescendo she climaxed, a dense cloud of pleasure wrapping itself around her.

He fingered her pussy harder, licking, nibbling her lips with his teeth, chasing the wave as it slowly fell back until finally he took his face and fingers from her swollen pussy.

She lay there in a daze, letting her mind catch up to her

body. She floated on light as she heard him stand and the soft clang of his belt buckle as he slid off his pants.

She sat up. "Your turn," she told him. "I want to taste you."

His eyebrows went up, especially as she leaned forward and took his cock in her hand. She motioned with her head for him to take a seat.

She loved the velvet softness of his cock against her fingers. She loved the way his breath caught just a little when she moved her fingers along his shaft. His stomach tightened with anticipation as she sank to her knees in front of him, the muscles clearly defined in a six pack.

She flicked her tongue on his head, then ran it down his shaft, lifting him and licking down the thick vein, down to his balls. She pressed his cock up against his own abdomen, looking up at him as she kissed and licked his balls. His groan was music to her ears.

"Does that feel good?" she asked, mumbling into his balls.

His cock twitched in her hand, making her smile.

She dragged her face along the bottom of his cock. When his head reached her wet lips she took him into her mouth.

She bobbed her head, toying with her tongue and twisting her hand on its thick base. With a wet pop she took him back out of her mouth, her saliva running in strings from her lips.

"Does that feel good?" she asked him, trying a naïve voice, to see if he'd like that. His cock responded with a powerful twitch. "Do you want me to keep sucking it?"

"Yes," he groaned. His hands went to her hair, tangling in the curls. He tugged at it, keeping her in control as she pleasured him.

She took him in her mouth again, running her tongue under him, guiding its swollen, velvety head along the top of her mouth, back towards her throat. She held him there, sucking harder. He clenched his ass and pushed into her, threatening her gag reflex. She smirked at him and cupped his balls, holding him firmly, sucking and running her tongue around him.

He tasted salty but a little sweet, a flavor she found she liked.

She set her fingers on her pussy, pushing the wet lips carefully. Having him in her mouth, groaning with pleasure, it was impossible not to want to feel the same. With her other hand she started tugging on the shaft of his cock again. As she sucked on his head she rubbed her clit in little circles.

She rubbed herself to the same rhythm that she bobbed her head up and down on his cock. He was right, it made his cock feel better in her mouth, and she felt herself begin to tingle again. She rubbed herself more eagerly, wanting to feel that rush of light, and in turn became more greedy on his cock. She reached under his sack, lifting it and then wrapping her fingers around him to make an 'O' that held his cock and balls snugly together.

She opened her jaw and let him push his cock into the back of her throat. She prepared for the moment his head went too far and resisted the urge to gag. She felt her saliva run down him as he throbbed in her mouth, her lips almost touching his balls. She bobbed her head up and down in little wet sucking motions.

He put his hands on her face and pulled his cock from her mouth.

"I want to fuck that tight little pussy." His eyes were wild, his patience receding.

"Mmm," she said. She started lying down on her back, her legs spread around him.

"No," he said. He shifted the weight of his body to the side, and with his strength lifted her, rolled her over quickly. He grabbed a pillow and stuffed it under her belly. She lay prone, arching her ass up. She turned, wanting to see what he was doing.

He was on his knees behind her, her legs beneath him, her round little ass pointed up at him.

"Not in my ass," she said, suddenly apprehensive.

He laughed. "No, not in your ass."

He reached between her thighs, spreading them a little wider and rubbing his finger against her pussy. His other hand took his meaty cock in hand and rubbed it on her wet swollen lips.

"Stop teasing and fuck me." She had to feel him inside of her, now.

With a push, he entered her, stopping just as soon as he was inside. The sensation was different, not as pleasurable as when he licked and fingered her, but it felt good in another way. He pressed his weight down, his hands gripping her ass cheeks, pushing and squeezing them roughly as his knees pinched her legs closer together.

With every inch, she found her body stretching to accommodate him. She knew that she'd be sore in the morning, but for now, she just gripped the bed spread and tried to enjoy it.

"God that pussy is so tight," he said. She could feel herself, snug as a glove around him. He rocked his hips, pushing deeper into her. She relaxed, let him penetrate her. His weight and muscle pressing down hard on her little body felt good, mixing with the small pain his thickness gave her virgin pussy.

"Fuck me," she moaned, laying her face down on the comforter, letting herself go limp, letting him fuck her however he wanted to.

He rolled his hips into her, his hands playing with her round ass. Squeezing it, giving it light spanks that tingled through her hips into her pussy. His cock filled her perfectly, stretched her and rubbed her. He thrust harder, the pain almost a pleasure of its own now.

She lifted herself up on her elbows, turning around to watch him fuck her. It was possibly the hottest, sexiest thing she'd ever seen in her life. Watching him push into her, his face concentrated on his own pleasure nearly sent her spiraling.

Jackson Weathers, billionaire CEO and known playboy, was enjoying her. He was enjoying her. He had fucked the hottest women in the world and was finding her sexier than them. She felt like a sex goddess.

He groaned with pleasure, staring down at her ass again, starting to thrust himself harder into her. She felt his balls press against the tops of her thighs as he settled deeper, shifted his weight onto her thighs, his thick cock burrowing more deeply, rubbing and nudging, pulsing.

She felt herself begin to tingle again, that rolling swell of heat and electricity. She was going to cum, but this one would be different. It was coming from somewhere else inside of her.

He must have felt her clench his cock tighter, because he grew more wild, lowering his hips with more force down onto her, shaking her little body with every thrust, Her thighs clenched. A flood of heat filled her, her fluids gushing around his thrusting cock. He pulled out, and she cried out with the sudden loss of his cock. However, his hand went to her clit, immediately causing new waves of pleasure to roll through her.

Her pleasure only spurred him on. He immediately re-entered her, pounding away at her now soaking wet pussy. His hand went to her shoulder, holding her down as he continued to use her body. He couldn't speak anymore, his body lost to the primal pleasure of finding release in her.

She wanted it. She wanted him to explode inside of her,

bringing her along for the ride. The idea of him loosing himself so completely within her caused her body to tighten around him, increasing the pleasure until he lost control.

He pushed down hard on her upper back, forcing her back to the bed. Every thrust was primal now. He was lost to a world of pleasure that she created. She groaned, enjoying every second of knowing that she was the cause of his pleasure.

She felt him speed up, felt him swell up within her. With a grunt he came hard. Thick ropes of semen splashed in her interior, and she felt her body open up to his orgasm. She felt his seed race up toward her fertile fields, looking for soil in which to plant new life. For a moment, she wanted nothing else, nothing but his semen to make a new life inside of her.

He continued thrusting, continued spraying inside of her, until he collapsed against her. His muscular chest felt good against her back, and she could feel the last few drops collecting by her entrance. Even that would be enough, she knew, to get her pregnant.

After a few moments, he pulled out of her and knelt up. He sat back, staring down at her, admiring his work. Admiring her body, filthy now with his seed.

Her hair stuck to her forehead. She was covered in sweat.

He rolled on to his back on the bed, staring at the ceiling while he caught his breath.

"That was better than in the back seat of the limo," he gasped.

"Way better," she agreed. "And, this way, once you've recovered, we can go again."

"You think I have that kind of stamina?" he asked, rolling onto his side and smiling at her.

"You are a billionaire," she replied. She grinned at him. "And, I have heard rumors about billionaires and their refractory periods."

He chuckled and pulled her into him, his arm strong and safe around her.

"Then I guess I'll just have to show you how true those rumors are," he murmured. He was already getting hard again.

ackson

"You look very nice, Mr. Weathers," Mrs. Bales said, looking up from her desk as he passed. She paused typing a memo to smile at him. "Are you going on a date with that lovely Ms. Emma?"

At the sound of Emma's name, Jackson couldn't help but smile. "No. Business dinner."

"Oh, that's right. It's Tuesday." His secretary nodded and then stood up. "Let me fix your tie. It's crooked."

Mrs. Bales hobbled around her desk, mumbling something about getting to the doctor for another look at her hips. She stood before her employer and fixed his tie for him. She smiled as she smoothed the dark silk of his tie.

"There you go," she said. "I sent the flowers to your house as instructed. I went with amaryllis because they mean, 'worth beyond beauty.'"

"Where did you learn that?" Jackson asked her.

"I looked it up," Mrs. Bales replied. "I do know how to use Google. I made sure that the flower meaning card got put in there too, so Emma will know as well."

"You're going to make her think I'm romantic," he scolded her with a smile. "Everyone knows that isn't me."

"I've seen the way you look at her," Mrs. Bales told him. "There's a secret between the two of you, but you look at her like she's worth something. I haven't seen you look at any of your other dates like that."

"It's how I look at you," he replied, kissing his secretary's cheek. She had been his secretary for longer than he could remember.

"You big liar." She smiled as she gave him a gentle push. "Now get going. You're going to be late."

"But at least I look good," he smiled, pointing to his tie. She rolled her eyes and went back behind her desk to keep working.

Jackson was in good spirits as he rode the elevator down. He glanced over at the coffee shop as he walked out the building. He was looking for Emma, even though he knew she wasn't working. It was just habit now. He wondered just how often he had looked over to her without realizing it.

He drove quickly to the steakhouse where he was meeting with a client. He followed the hostess to the back table where Mr. Cannon waited.

"You're late," Mr. Cannon announced. He already had two empty drink glasses on the table.

"I'm right on time," Jackson replied. "You just like my free drinks."

"I have no idea what you're talking about," Mr. Cannon said. He caught the hostess' attention. "Another drink please."

Jackson simply laughed. This was how this meeting always went.

It was his monthly meeting with Cannon Chemicals. They always met at this particular steakhouse, and ate and drank until they could barely move. Jackson would then pick up some beautiful girl at the bar, take her upstairs to the penthouse suite of the hotel, and have a wonderful evening.

Except that wasn't going to happen tonight.

The thought surprised Jackson as he settled into his regular spot and had the regular conversation. He could see a stunning blonde sitting at the bar, but he had no desire to talk to her.

He wanted to go home and talk with Emma. He wanted to bring Emma up to the penthouse suite.

"Jackson, you feeling okay?"

Jackson shook his head, realizing that he wasn't paying attention to his friend. "Sorry, just thinking."

"You were thinking of that sexy little brunette you found," Mr. Cannon decided. The man grinned at him. "I can't blame you. When you get tired of her, would you give her my number?"

Jackson's hand balled into a fist and he nearly punched Mr. Cannon right in the nose. How dare he talk about Emma that way?

Luckily, Jackson caught himself before he got past making the fist. He smiled and took a calming breath.

"You'll be waiting a long time," he told the other man. "I think I'm going to hold onto this one."

Mr. Cannon laughed like Jackson had told the world's most hilarious joke. "You? I'll believe it when I see it."

Jackson willed himself to uncurl his fingers. There was no reason to be angry. Mr. Cannon wasn't saying anything bad about Emma, or Jackson. It was the idea that Jackson would leave her that made him angry.

Even Jackson could admit that with his track record, it

was a fair assumption to make. He wasn't sure why hearing it out loud made him so angry.

"So, onto business," Jackson announced. He needed to stop thinking about Emma. He needed to concentrate on his business.

"If you say so," Mr. Cannon replied. He motioned for another drink as the waitress walked by.

Two hours later, the meeting was over.

You home? Jackson texted Emma. He could already imagine himself finding her naked in his bed when he walked home. He rather liked that option.

Babysitting Sammy. I'll be home in an hour, Emma replied.

Jackson sighed. He didn't want to go home without her there.

Jackson didn't know quite what to do with himself. All his regular habits were thrown off. He wouldn't be going upstairs to the penthouse suite with a leggy blonde, but he didn't want to go home to an empty house, either.

So, he went to the bar and got a drink. One more drink, and he would head home. He could take his time and get there around the same time Emma would. The idea made him happy.

"Hello, stranger," a sensual voice purred from behind him. A soft touch ran across his shoulders.

"Katy." Jackson recognized the voice and the soft touch. Standing next to him in a gown made for sliding to the floor, was Katy. She was often the leggy blonde that went upstairs with him after these meetings.

"I was in town and thought I might find you here," she purred, sliding onto the bar stool next to him. Everything about her oozed sex. From her exposed cleavage to the way she kept her legs pointed directly at him, she wanted him.

But for the first time in his life, he didn't want her.

Any red-blooded male with a heartbeat should have swooped Katy up and taken what she willingly offered. The woman was sex appeal walking, and an eager and willing partner, but Jackson couldn't find the desire to sleep with her.

He didn't want her.

It was a very strange feeling.

"I'm sorry, but I'm not interested tonight, Katy," Jackson said, the words forming strangely in his mouth.

Katy's eyes went wide. "What?"

"I said I'm not interested tonight," Jackson repeated. It was easier the second time.

Katy blinked rapidly. She had probably never heard those words in her life. "Are you serious?"

She crossed her arms, showing off her massive, half-covered breasts, and pouted. Her red lips looked primed for sucking and kissing.

And he didn't care.

Jackson chuckled and stood up, leaving his drink half finished on the bar. "Yeah. I am. Have a great night."

He tossed some money on the counter for his half-finished drink. He didn't want it anymore. A thought hit him. Flowers for Emma.

Only, more. More than just a single bouquet. A whole flower shop. He wanted to see her smile. He had an hour to pull it off.

"Come on, Jackson," Katy purred, putting her hand on his chest. "Stay with me. We always have such a good time."

He gently took her hand away. "Goodnight, Katy. Don't ask again."

He left the restaurant and went home to surprise Emma with an apartment full of flowers. He couldn't wait to see her smile.

140

mma

Something was different. Emma wasn't sure what it was, but as she woke up that morning, she knew something had changed.

She slowly opened her eyes and looked around. She was in Jackson's bed, wrapped up in gray linen that felt smooth against her bare skin. Jackson was nowhere to be seen. She relaxed back into her pillow and sighed.

He was probably already at work. She on the other hand, felt like she could roll over and fall right back to sleep. Despite the fact that she had slept like a rock, she was exhausted.

"Too much sex," she mumbled into the pillow. That had to be the reason she was so tired. It was either that or she was getting sick. She really hoped it was just too much amazing sex and she just needed to get in better shape.

She groaned, unable to fall back asleep despite wanting

to. With a sigh and a groan, she sat up and swung her legs to the edge of the bed. She was so freaking tired, but yet unable to sleep more. Maybe coffee would make her feel better.

Her feet hit the fluffy rug and she reached for her robe hanging by the bed. It had taken her a few nights to become comfortable with sleeping in the nude. She'd mostly accepted it because it was so wonderful to simply cuddle into Jackson's arms and fall asleep after one of their epic lovemaking sessions.

It was so much nicer than leaving him to put on pajamas.

She padded out to the kitchen, eyes still blurry with sleep. She secretly hoped that Jackson would still be in the kitchen. He liked to read the paper in the morning and sip his coffee. She liked finding him and joining him for a shared comfortable, quiet morning.

He wasn't there. Emma sighed and wondered what was bothering her. Something was different and she couldn't put her finger on it. She had felt it a few days ago, but the feeling was stronger now.

The coffee pot hummed to life as she pressed the buttons. Jackson had the fanciest coffee machine she'd ever seen. It was a good thing she had worked in a coffee shop with a temperamental espresso machine, or she would have never been able to figure out how to work the dang thing.

In just a few seconds, Emma had a cup of steaming coffee complete with foamed milk and just a dash of vanilla. It was heaven in a cup.

She wrapped her hands around the mug and sat down at the table. She was a little more awake now, but still tired. It was a good thing she didn't have to work today, or any day really, because she wasn't sure she would make it to the end of the day without a nap.

She sipped her coffee and sat in the sunshine pouring in

through the big windows. She could understand why cats loved sunshine windows. They were decadent.

The smell of roses caught her attention and she smiled. The entire living room was filled with different colors of the beautiful blossoms. She still couldn't believe Jackson had filled a room with roses for her to walk into when she came home.

She'd actually been glad he'd video taped the whole thing on his phone. He'd even put it live on Facebook for everyone to see. At first, she felt a little used. He was showing off their relationship for the public, but then, that *was* what she'd signed up for. It was a good idea to share it.

Especially when she watched it later and saw how happy she was. She'd grinned like an idiot through the whole thing. It was when she watched it alone that she caught his smile in the hallway mirror. He hadn't meant to catch himself smiling, but she saw his reflection in the hallway mirror as he recorded her. The way he smiled at her made her heart pitter-patter, even if it was a show for others. His smile made her feel like it wasn't all fake.

Her phone buzzed from her robe pocket with a notification. Emma pulled out her phone and saw that she needed to turn in her monthly work hours requests. She chuckled and turned the notification off. She'd forgotten to do it when she quit her job just over a month ago. There was no need to submit her schedule now.

She sipped her coffee, enjoying the sunshine for a moment.

And then she nearly spit it out.

She was late.

She hastily pulled up her calendar and did the mental math. Her last period was six weeks ago. She'd been living with Jackson for almost a month. She was officially two weeks late.

Could she be pregnant already?

Her hands shook as she set down the phone and pushed her coffee away.

Without meaning to, her hands went to her belly. Was there life in there now? New, tiny life? Her stomach felt the same, but she'd known something was different when she woke up this morning.

She knew something had changed.

Emma swallowed hard. There was only one way to be certain.

She put on a pair of jean shorts and a comfortable t-shirt, threw her hair up in a ponytail, and grabbed her purse. On a last minute decision, she put on a ball cap and some reflective sunglasses. There was a corner store just a couple of blocks away that would have pregnancy tests.

She thought about just calling for someone to get her one. It would be easy in this apartment, and Jackson had told her she could ask for anything to be delivered. She thought about it, and then decided against it.

First, she'd have to find something to do while she waited for them. If she went to the store herself, she would have something to keep her busy. Second, she didn't want Jackson to know yet. If it was just a false alarm, she didn't want him to ask about it.

If it wasn't a false alarm...

She wasn't sure what to do.

"He wants the baby," she said under her breath as she waved to the doorman and headed out into the summer sunshine. It was still early, so the heat was comfortable without being oppressive.

This was the contract. This was what was supposed to happen. Jackson would be thrilled that she was pregnant so easily.

So why was she nervous?

She stood at a streetlight and waited for her turn to cross the street. Why was her stomach in knots and her palms sweating?

She nearly missed the light change as it dawned on her.

She was terrified because it was real now. She really cared about him, and if she was pregnant, then they would be tied together forever. She knew she would always love him. She'd loved him from the moment he'd walked into her coffee shop years ago.

She hurried across the street, ignoring the blare of horns as the light changed. She needed to get to the store as soon as possible. She needed to know for sure.

She felt like sprinting to the store, but that wouldn't work. For starters, she was still tired, and the other reason was that she didn't want to draw attention to herself. She was the girlfriend of a billionaire about to buy a pregnancy test.

It wouldn't be a bad thing if it got out, since the baby was part of the master plan, but she wanted to be the one to tell him. She didn't want him finding out because of some trashy gossip column. She wanted to stick to the plan as much as she could for the moment.

The corner store was quiet. The clerk barely glanced up as Emma walked in. She wandered around the store for a moment, trying to get her hands to stop shaking. She picked up the test, a bottle of water, and a pack of gum. It felt strange to just buy the test.

"This all?" The clerk didn't even look at her. He just stared at his computer screen, looking incredibly bored.

"Yeah." She glanced around and saw her face on at least three magazines. They were all the trashy tabloids, but there she was, standing next to Jackson. "And these," she added.

The clerk shrugged and added on the magazines. Emma knew it was a bad idea to read them. They wouldn't say anything she didn't already know, but she couldn't help herself.

She tugged her hat down lower when the clerk gave her the total. She flipped the magazines over so she wasn't visible as soon as she could.

"Thank you. Come again." The clerk sounded like a recording. Emma nodded and gathered her things together and hurried out of the store.

Back out in the sunlight, Emma felt like she'd just pulled off the biggest heist in history. The clerk hadn't recognized her or even commented on the test. Her hands shook with relief. Step one was done.

Now it was time to take the test.

Emma paused. She didn't want to take it at his apartment. The maids would see it when they cleaned up. She thought about using her apartment, but the maids cleaned that one too. She didn't even know where the dumpster was in the building.

Emma stood on the sidewalk and chewed on her cheek.

With a deep breath she turned around and went back inside the shop.

"Where's the bathroom?" she asked the clerk.

He sighed and pointed toward the back corner. She nodded and headed back there, really hoping that he was still disinterested.

The bathroom was tiny, but at least it looked clean. Emma took the test out of the box and read the directions three times before feeling semi-confident that she could do this properly. It didn't seem hard- just pee on a stick- but the last thing she wanted to do was mess it up and have to buy another test.

She took a deep breath, prepped the stick and did her best.

Peeing on a stick is not an easy feat. It seems like it should be, but it does require a unique hand-eye-pee coordination that not every woman has practiced.

Emma made sure the applicator had enough before carefully balancing the precious test on the sink while she cleaned up. She had to wait a few minutes for the test results anyway, so she was glad she had something to do.

She checked her watch every five seconds. The test said it could take up to three minutes for a result with a possible positive marker at the minute mark.

Fifty-four, fifty-five, fifty-six....

The seconds took hours.

At the one minute mark, Emma picked up the test. It was early, but she couldn't wait any longer.

Her breath caught and she wasn't sure if she was going to laugh or cry.

Two pink lines.

She was pregnant.

 mma

"Are you okay?"

"What?" Emma stuttered, turning from the limo window and looking blankly at Jackson.

"You're distracted," he told her. "I've asked you the same question three times and you haven't said a word. You just sat there. Are you okay?"

"Oh, I'm sorry," Emma replied. She reached for his hand. "I'm just tired."

"Are you sick?" Jackson asked. "You look a little pale."

"I'm fine," Emma told him. "It's probably just a little bug. I'll be fine."

A baby bug, she thought to herself. *And I'll be fine in about nine months.*

Emma thought about telling him about the positive pregnancy test, but decided to wait until she had it confirmed by a doctor. Her appointment was in a couple of days. She was still so early in her pregnancy that she didn't want to get his hopes up yet.

She didn't want him to think about his business troubles tonight, either, so, she was waiting until the doctor confirmed what the pregnancy test told her. It was better for everyone that way.

"Oh look, we're here," Emma announced, pointing to the stadium. She was glad for the distraction. The way Jackson was looking at her made her nervous. She was going to have to focus on him tonight.

The limo pulled up to the front gate of Stingray Baseball Stadium. Tonight was going to be a great game against the hated Redbirds. The stands were already nearing capacity, yet more and more people in Stingray blue and gold kept coming in.

The limo door opened and Emma stepped out. The smells of peanuts, beer, and popcorn filled her nose. Thank god she wasn't having morning sickness yet, or it would have been terrible. She sighed with relief.

"This way," Jackson said, taking her hand. He guided her to a private entrance and then over to a hidden elevator. Two security guards checked them out before allowing them inside. From there, they went straight up and to the best seats in the entire stadium.

She followed Jackson as he led her to the tunnel that the players used to access the field, but instead of heading out onto the field he made a right hand turn at a doorway. Inside was the most impressive seats she'd ever seen for a sporting event.

Four leather recliners sat in a beautiful room looking out at the field. Except, she was so close to the field that she could almost touch the players. The umpire squatted only three feet away from her and she was close enough to see the stitching on the balls when he set them down.

It was as close to being a major league baseball player as she was ever going to get.

"Wow," Emma whispered, standing next to the window and looking out at the field. Any closer and she'd need to wear cleats. "I didn't even know there were seats like this."

"You said you liked baseball games," Jackson replied, settling into one of the recliner chairs.

"Yeah, but I usually get the nosebleed seats," Emma said, turning to smile at him. "You know, the ones the grocery stores say you 'won' for buying enough groceries that month?"

"I can get you one of those seats." Jackson moved like he was getting up.

"No, nope. This is good, I'm happy," she assured him. He grinned and relaxed back in his seat.

Jackson pressed a button on the side of the chair. Within seconds, there was a polite knock on the door and a man in a blue and gold polo shirt opened the door.

"How can I help you?" the man asked. "My name is Joe, and I'll be your private service tonight."

"Hello Joe," Jackson greeted him. "I'll have my usual."

"Of course, Mr. Weathers. It's always a pleasure to have you here," Joe replied warmly. He turned to Emma. "And for you, miss?"

"Um, what do you have?" Emma asked. She was used to shelling out ten bucks for a single foamy cup of beer at these games, but beer wasn't something she should be drinking today.

Joe quickly handed her a menu that was four pages thick. Every beer Emma could think of was listed, along with wine, mixed drinks, sodas, and every food she'd ever seen offered in the stadium and then some.

"I'll have a ginger ale and some of the Stingray Special fries," she said after a moment.

"Excellent choice," Joe replied. "I'll have those right down."

"Joe's the best," Jackson told Emma as the door swung shut behind their server. "I always request him for these games."

Before Emma had a chance to respond, Joe was back with a large beer and hot dog for Jackson and the soda and fries for Emma. She wasn't sure how he'd gotten them so fast. He wasn't even out of breath.

"Can I get you anything else?" Joe asked, smiling at the two of them.

"No," Jackson replied. He held the hot dog and smiled as he took a bite. "Perfect as always, Joe."

"Please let me know if you need anything," Joe told them. He nodded politely and disappeared behind the door again.

"Does he just wait out there for us to call him?" Emma asked, looking at the door.

"I'm not sure what he does," Jackson replied, his mouth full of food. "Come sit down. The game's about to start."

Emma took her food and drink and sat down in the comfortable chairs. She could see everything. It made the baseball game so much more fun when she was in the same position as the umpire to call strike or ball. In just a couple of innings she was yelling at the glass when she disagreed with the umpire.

"You should slow down on those drinks," Jackson teased. "I think they're going to your head."

"It's just ginger ale," she scoffed. Then she blushed. "I'm getting a little animated, aren't I?"

Jackson chuckled. "You're having fun."

She grinned at him and sat back down. "Thank you for this. I'm having a lot of fun." She leaned over and kissed his cheek.

"Well, as long as you're having a good time, you should

check out the mega-tron," Jackson told her, pointing to the giant TV for the stadium.

Emma frowned slightly, but looked to where he pointed. In big letters she slowly read the words that she knew she'd never forget.

EMMA SHERIDAN, WILL YOU MARRY ME?

"Jackson?" Emma turned from the TV to find Jackson down on one knee. He had a small black box open to her with the biggest diamond Emma had ever seen in her life.

"Emma Sheridan, will you marry me?" he asked, a confident grin on his face.

Emma stood there for a moment in shock. She hadn't seen this coming. Jackson had been so comfortable and completely at ease all evening. He hadn't looked even the slightest bit nervous about proposing.

He wasn't nervous because she was contractually obligated to say yes.

There was no doubt of her answer, so there were no nerves. This was a business transaction, albeit a pleasant one.

She'd known from the moment she signed that contract what was coming. They'd never agreed to love. This was all about appearances and saving his diaper company.

So why did the fact that this wasn't real hurt so much?

Why did she want it to be real?

"Emma?" Jackson prompted. He held up the ring a little higher to catch the sparkle. It was then that she realized they were on the mega-tron. She was glad she'd worn something cute.

"Yes," she said, putting on a big, bright smile. "Oh my god, YES!"

She could play her part just like him. She could pretend that this proposal was a total surprise and that she was over the moon.

It was why she was getting paid. She could keep her feelings to herself. Just because she was falling for Jackson, just because she wished that he could have been a little nervous, didn't mean she couldn't smile.

Outside, the crowd went wild. Players came and banged on the glass and the crowd screamed their approval. Jackson carefully slid the ring onto her finger, kissed her, and then held her in his arms.

The tears in her eyes were happy tears, at least according to the people watching. No one would ever know that this was fake, and that was why she was crying.

"You're doing great," he whispered in her ear. "Everyone totally believes us."

"Yeah, great." Emma sniffled and was glad she didn't have to look him in the eyes right now. She just tucked her head into his shoulder like she was overwhelmed with emotion. At least that wasn't far from the truth.

Outside, the crowd finally calmed down and the game continued into the next inning. Jackson released her from his hug and grinned.

"I think I surprised you," he said with a chuckle.

She wiped a tear from her cheek. "Yeah. You sure did."

"Do you like the ring?" Now he sounded a little nervous. This was something that wasn't in the contract.

"It's beautiful," she replied, finally taking a good look at it. The band appeared to be white gold with a single princess cut diamond sparkling in a delicate setting. The diamond looked like it belonged in a museum with a full time guard, it was so big. She had no doubt it was real. Jackson was a billionaire after all.

Jackson grinned and his shoulders relaxed. She leaned into him and he wrapped his arm around her. It felt nice. For a moment, she could almost believe this was real. She could almost believe that he wanted to marry her.

Almost.

"Are you sure you're okay?" Jackson asked, looking concerned.

"Of course. Why?" Emma replied. She put on her best smile.

"Because you're still crying." Jackson frowned. Tears obviously weren't his thing.

Emma chuckled. "They're happy tears. It's an emotional moment. I just had a billionaire propose to me. Life is good."

Jackson's concerned look slowly faded. "Okay. I'm glad you're happy."

"Definitely," she assured him, snuggling into his shoulder a little more. His arm felt good wrapped around her. Even though their relationship wasn't real, she could pretend it was. For this moment, she could pretend she was happily in love and that nothing was wrong in the world.

At the end of the ninth inning, the Stingrays were winning. It was the perfect way to end the day, Emma decided. She was engaged and her favorite team was going to win.

The game ended and the players all came out on the field to shake hands. It surprised Emma that the stands were still mostly full. No one appeared to have left, despite the fact that the game was over. That was when the fireworks started.

Big blossoms of color lit up the stadium followed by thunderous booms. Emma gasped with delight and stood from her chair, pushing her nose into the glass and watching the sky. Blue, gold, green, purple, and streaks of silver all sparkled against the dark night.

But there was more. Two red streaks flew across the sky and exploded into heart shapes. A third heart appeared, followed by what was clearly the letters J and E written in fireworks. Then the letter W and more hearts.

Emma turned and looked back at Jackson. He was grinning at her, obviously enjoying her childlike delight at the fireworks.

"Did you have them do that?" Emma asked, turning back to watch the colors lighting the sky. She'd never seen fireworks this good, even on the Fourth of July.

Jackson came and stood beside her at the window, putting his arm around her and looking up at the night sky as color blossomed and bloomed.

"I thought you would like it," he said softly.

She turned to see the colors glimmering in his green eyes. He made her knees turn to jelly and her stomach heat. For a moment, she forgot everything. There was nothing in the world that could be more beautiful than the way he looked at her. Not even fireworks.

The fireworks came to an end with a brilliant display of light. Hearts made of red and blue filled the sky once again, and the thunder of the fireworks deafened everything. The crowd cheered, chanting "Weathers" throughout the stadium.

For a moment, Emma let herself believe that this was real. That he'd done the fireworks and the proposal simply for her, and not for the publicity it would bring his company. Deep down, she knew this was all a show, but she wanted it to be real.

She looked over at the handsome man beside her.

Even if this was all pretend, even if she'd lost her heart to someone who didn't return her feelings, this was a pretty amazing way to live.

mma

"Did I surprise you?" Jackson asked. He reached over and took her hand, checking to make sure the ring fit her finger as they walked down the empty corridor toward their private entrance. It was strange not having to fight the crowds.

"Yes," she told him with a grin. "I didn't see it coming at all. You did good."

He smiled, pleased with his success. He held her hand as they walked out of the stadium and directly into the limo. It took Emma a moment to realize just how quickly they'd gotten out of the stadium.

Private parking at the stadium certainly had its perks. Emma was used to waiting for the stadium to clear, waiting in the aisles as everyone filed out of the stands and tried to remember where they parked. It usually took at least thirty minutes to get out of the parking lot due to the sheer volume of people.

Because of Jackson, they were out of the stadium and on the highway in less than ten minutes. Emma didn't even know that was possible until tonight. There were a lot of things she didn't know money could buy, but she was finding out.

Emma looked down at the sparkly gem on her finger. It looked out of place on her regular hand. This was something that was meant for a princess or a movie star. She was just a normal girl.

"It looks good on you," Jackson told her. "I rather like knowing that you're mine."

A hot flush traveled through her and she looked at the rock a little differently. This was a sign that she was Jackson's. She liked knowing that he wanted her. That he had picked this out to mark her as his partner.

She leaned over and kissed him. She'd meant the kiss to be small and chaste. Just a peck on the lips. But he caught her head in his hands and pressed her to him. Her mouth opened for more of him and he happily obliged.

When she pulled away, she was panting and the heat in her core was growing. She licked her lips and grinned.

"I believe you promised me something," she told him.

He frowned slightly. "And that was?"

She leaned over, putting her mouth next to his ear and whispered. "Sex in a limo."

A slow smile crossed his face, crooked and cocky. "I did, didn't I?"

She nodded slowly, her own grin growing to match his. He reached over and raised the privacy screen, the two of them smiling at one another like little devils as it raised. She knew that the driver probably knew exactly what was going on back here, but she could pretend that he was oblivious.

Besides, now that it was up, Jackson was looking at her like she was delicious and that he hadn't eaten in a week. His pupils dilated as he looked her over. "Come here."

Emma moved with as much grace as the car would allow. She didn't sit next to him. She straddled his lap, her skirt straining at the hem and riding up her ass as she put her knees on either side of his waist.

Jackson's hands went to her ass, pulling the skirt up and around her waist. He groaned his approval at finding only a tiny thong under her skirt.

"Do you wear these things just to drive me wild?" he asked, his fingers digging into her ass.

She didn't answer, instead pulling the Stingray jersey over her head and showing off her matching lacy bra.

"I matched on purpose," she told him as his eyes went to her breasts. "But I was thinking you'd see it more at home."

"I'm glad I didn't have to wait," he murmured, tipping his head forward and kissing the tops of her breasts peeking out of the lacy cups. "If I'd known this was what you were wearing, we would have done this on the way here."

She chuckled softly as he buried his face into her cleavage. She could feel him hardening between her legs and the ache between her own intensified. Her hips rocked, her clit searching for stimulation and the rest of her body waiting to be filled.

Jackson released her ass and undid his belt buckle. She figured out what he was doing and raised herself up, still kissing him as he undid his pants and slid them down. Before lowering herself, she broke the kiss and reached down.

He bulged in his briefs, hard and ready for her. Her breath caught with desire as she caressed him through the thin fabric. Her blood heated as she touched him and his cock jumped under her touch.

"Emma," he whispered, her name a plea for more. She grinned and moved the fabric to the side, releasing his cock into the air.

It always amazed her how large he was. She had a hard time believing how perfectly he fit inside of her, given just how wide and long he was. It was probably why he was so good at making her feel good.

With his cock free, all that stood in the way was her panties. Jackson gave her a wolfish, hungry grin as she moved them to the side and hovered over him.

She held there for a moment, hovering on the precipice of pleasure. Their eyes connected, Jackson's green ones full of lust and directed entirely on her. He gripped her hips, but didn't force her down. He was enjoying the tension as much as she was.

The limo hit a small bump and Emma went up, and then down. She gasped with the suddenness of it. Her body cried out in pleasure as he filled her to the brim. Jackson groaned, his hands tightening on her hips.

Together they began to rock and writhe against one another. He filled her so completely that she was sure she would burst. He looked at her like she was the most beautiful creature on the planet. Underneath them, the limo swayed and bumped along the road, adding an extra level to their motions.

Emma arched her back, working her body up and down along his shaft. Jackson groaned, tipping his head back and his eyes rolling into the back of his head. His hands clenched on her hips and his stomach tightened as she worked her magic.

"More," he whispered, his voice ragged with desire.

Emma obliged, upping her hip undulations and watching his face contort with pleasure. She loved the way he felt inside of her. The eternal ache in her core almost vanished when he was inside of her, but the only way it was ever satisfied was with his seed.

"We're almost home, sir," the driver said over the intercom. Jackson met Emma's eyes. They needed to finish this.

He pulled her from his hips and she went to her hands and knees on the limo seat. It was tight and her shoulder pressed into the seat back, but she could hold it. Jackson went to his knees behind her, his fingers on her ass for a moment as he guided himself into her.

She loved this position. Doggy-style had a naughty feel to it, plus she loved that she could waggle her ass at him. She loved that she could arch her back and take in more of him.

He slapped her ass, the sound ringing out in the interior of the limo. His breath came harder and faster, as did his thrusts.

"Come in me," she whispered. She didn't have to worry about getting pregnant anymore, but she still felt the desire to have him inside of her.

Jackson's body went tight and she felt him swell deep inside of her. His life force sped from him, coating her insides with life-giving fluid. She took it all, milking him with her muscles for every drop. She wanted it. Needed it. It was the only thing that would quench the fire within her.

Jackson's breathing was ragged and heavy as the car pulled to a stop. They both panted with effort. Emma came to her senses first, spinning on the seat to come to a normal position. She lifted her hips and pulled her panties back into place as well as her skirt.

Jackson pulled up his pants and redid his belt as she searched for her shirt on the floor. She found it only a little wrinkled as she pulled it up and over her head.

Jackson grinned and kissed her cheek. "How was that?"

"Better than promised," she told him. "But..."

He frowned. "But what?"

She grinned. "I think I'll need another time at it. We need to go for a long drive one of these days."

Jackson's frown disappeared, replaced by a hungry smile. "Sounds good to me."

ackson

"Sales are up for the first time in months," Jane announced, tossing a report onto Jackson's desk. She grinned widely as she stood before him in his office. He picked up the stack of papers and flipped through it.

"It's hardly anything," he scoffed, setting it down. "It's not something to brag about."

"Come on, you're smarter than that," she assured him. "Think about the second derivative. Sales velocity. We stopped the downward slide and changed direction. It's huge. It means that what we are doing is working."

"You mean Emma?" Jackson asked. He couldn't help the small smile that crossed his lips when he said her name.

"Yes, Emma," Jane agreed. "I don't know where you found her, but I want six of her. She's perfect. Pretty, but not unbelievable. Smart, but not overwhelming. And sweet. The paparazzi caught a shot of her with her friend's baby, and I could see the sales go up with every share it got."

"She is one of a kind," Jackson agreed.

"Yes." Jane's eyes narrowed. "You are not allowed to cheat on her for any reason. Do you understand me?"

Jackson's anger flared in the pit of his stomach. "Watch yourself," he warned.

Jane held up her hand. "Do you need your female history in pictures? The paparazzi have a list of every woman you've slept with this year. You even look at another woman, and that will be front page news. They're waiting for you to slip up."

Jackson frowned. "What do you mean?"

Jane sighed. "You're known as a player. You like women," Jane told him. "And you suddenly have this whirlwind romance with the coffee girl. There's a lot of unpleasant rumors swirling around about why that is."

"Such as?"

"You don't want to know," Jane assured him.

He raised his eyebrows and waited. "Yes, I do."

Jane pinched her mouth together before speaking. "She's blackmailing you. You're on drugs, or perhaps this is all a big sham."

"Because heaven forbid I actually fall in love." He hated that his stomach clenched and he felt sick at hearing anyone could think poorly of Emma. She would never blackmail anyone.

"Everyone loves a good love story," Jane told him. "But everyone loves to watch a train wreck even more. And, if you even glance at another woman before or immediately after your wedding, that will be a train wreck no one will want to look away from."

"Everyone likes Emma, but they like drama more,"

Jackson said, understanding perfectly. His jaw tightened and he wanted to hit something.

"Exactly," Jane confirmed. "So, I'm telling you that if you want this to work, you cannot give them the drama. You must keep the happy love story going. Can you do that?"

Jane stood in front of his desk, putting her hands wide and staring into his face. She looked at him, judging every motion, every twitch, and every inch of him.

"Yes," he promised. The word came smooth and clear. He was as sure that he could do this as he was that he could walk across his office without tripping. Stranger yet, he found himself *wanting* to do it. Emma was more than enough to keep him interested. There was no need to seek other women.

Jane watched him for another second. "Okay then." She stood up, apparently pleased with what she saw. She believed him.

"What comes next?" Jackson asked her.

"I need some photos of the two of you. I would also like some with her and that baby again. You too."

"Me? With the baby?" Jackson didn't do babies. Sure, they were cute in pictures. But in real life, they peed. And cried. And he wasn't quite sure how to hold them properly. Hell, they never even behaved for those cute pictures.

"Yes, you. You are still planning on having one, right?"

"Yes," Jackson said. The baby was still far away though. He had time. Emma wasn't pregnant yet, so it was fine.

"Then, we get a picture of you holding the baby and looking lovingly at Emma," Jane replied with a confident shrug. She smiled and her eyes went distant. "The focus groups will eat it up."

"If you say so. Schedule it with my secretary."

Jane's eyes came back into focus as she looked him over.

"You're different," she said, a slight frown creasing her forehead.

"I'm exactly the same," he assured her.

"No. You're happier. You've smiled more today than I think I've ever seen. You've kept your temper. If this is because of Emma, I change my order. I don't want just six of her anymore. I want a full dozen."

Jackson laughed. "Maybe I just like my business being successful."

Jane shook her head. "No, it's more than that. You're happy. Deep in your soul kind of happy."

"If you say so," Jackson replied, laughing her off. Jane shrugged, and left his office with a smile on her face.

As the door closed, Jackson wondered if Jane was right. Was he happier? Was it because of Emma?

He certainly looked forward to going home now. He didn't want to stay at the office until he couldn't see straight. He didn't want to go through his phone and find the numbers to the ballerinas he used to enjoy. He'd actually deleted all of them.

Now, if he wanted to see ballerinas, it was because he wanted to take Emma to the ballet.

He shook his head, trying to clear the strange thoughts. He was a playboy. That was who he was. He had accepted this a long time ago. He was never going to find love, but he was going to enjoy every moment of searching.

But what if he had found someone worth changing for? Someone to end the search?

He shook his head. He wasn't that lucky. That wasn't what the fates had in store for him. He was enjoying Emma. They were friends. He pushed away the warmth that grew around his heart when he thought of her.

It wasn't love. He wasn't the kind to fall in love.

He was just happy that everything was going to plan. Emma was working her bubbly, happy magic that would get mothers to trust his products again, and she made him smile. It was a win-win situation all around. *That's* why he was happy.

Jackson leaned back in his chair and smiled at the ceiling. With Emma helping him, what could possibly go wrong?

ackson

The rest of the work day went smooth as silk. Sales were up. Stocks were up. The investors were happy. The board of directors was happy. There was no talk of replacing him.

Plus, he was taking Emma out to dinner tonight. He knew this amazing little sushi place that could fit them in a back corner where no one would bother them. He was going to eat sushi and laugh with Emma until he burst.

Jackson's day couldn't be better.

"Mrs. Bales, have a fabulous evening," he called to his secretary as he left the office. The clock read just after five.

"You too, Mr. Weathers," Mrs. Bales called out after him. "I made those reservations you asked for. Everything is set, just like you requested."

Jackson turned and grinned at her. "Thank you."

"Of course, Mr. Weathers," she replied. "Give my best to Emma."

He was going to give Mrs. Bales a raise. That's how good of a day it was. He was going to give the whole damn company a raise if things continued this well. Sales were finally coming back up. W&W BabyCo no longer had to catch up to the Innocence Company.

Jessica Balboa and her company could shove it. W&W BabyCo was here to stay. He walked across the company courtyard to get to the parking garage. After the air conditioned inside, the sun felt good. He reached for the heavy parking garage door, eager for the cool shadows and his expensive car.

"You know it's bad form for the CEO to leave work early," a snide voice remarked from the shadows.

Jackson turned to see Max Singleton leaning against the building. The man wore his button down shirt open to the summer evening, but still wore a suit jacket. Max Singleton had to look the part, even if it was roasting outside. Yet, somehow the man didn't seem to be sweating.

It was probably because Max came from the bowels of hell. To him, this summer evening probably felt cold.

"Max, what an unpleasant surprise," Jackson replied. He didn't slow down. He just kept on walking into the garage. He hoped that the door closing in Max's face would deter him, but it didn't. The man continued to follow him.

He wasn't sure how Max had gotten past security, but he was going to be having a very serious discussion with them tomorrow. He didn't appreciate being ambushed like this. He kept walking, but Max simply followed along.

"I'm sure you're wondering why I'm here. I was seeing a friend of mine in the building," Max said, as if they were having a conversation. "I'd heard rumors that the great Jackson Weathers was leaving the office early these days, but

I simply dismissed them as nonsense. Now I see I was mistaken."

"Do you want something?" Jackson asked, turning and stopping.

"I know it's fake," Max said. "Anyone with eyes can see it."

Jackson didn't even bother to respond. He simply rolled his eyes and kept walking.

"It's fake and I can prove it," Max shouted. The words echoed through the empty garage, bouncing off employee cars.

Jackson paused, even though he knew he shouldn't. He shouldn't let Max press his buttons. Today was a good day. The only reason Max was here was because sales were back up. He was taking customers away from the Innocence Company and Max didn't like it.

He didn't have to dignify this conversation. Jackson knew Max didn't have a thing on him. He couldn't. There was nothing Max *could* have.

Yet, still, he paused. Anger pulsed through him.

"Fuck you," he said, not bothering to turn around. The words came out harsh and guttural. He turned and looked at Max. "Fuck you."

"Oh, I think I touched a nerve." Max grinned like a Cheshire cat, his teeth gleaming in the parking garage gloom.

"You don't have shit," Jackson announced. "Because there isn't shit to have. Make up all the stories you want, Max. You are wrong this time."

"I am?" Max chuckled. "Katy might say differently."

"Katy?"

"The girl from the restaurant. I knew you slept around, but I thought you at least remembered your favorite's names," Max chided.

Jackson laughed. It was a full belly laugh. The sound

boomed through the garage. "That's your fucking proof? I didn't know you were so terrible at your job, Max."

Max's confident posture didn't change. "Katy says different. She says you took her up to your usual room, but at least you had the grace to call out Emma's name."

"I didn't know you were practicing for a stand-up comedian job," Jackson replied. "Because that's funny right there."

"You saying it isn't true?" Max grinned like he was winning.

"I'm saying that the hotel tapes will say it isn't true. I'm saying that my security camera in the elevator to my apartment will say it isn't true. I'm saying that my fiancée, who gave me the best damn blow job of my life that night, will say it isn't true."

"Except, Katy already told people," Max said with a shrug. "The first story is usually the one believed."

Jackson laughed again. "Seriously, you should book a time slot at a comedy club, because you are hilarious!" Jackson slapped his knee, like this was the funniest thing he'd heard all week.

"You think it won't damage you?" Max asked, still confident.

"No. You know why?" Jackson grinned and walked over, getting in Max's face. He was taller and heavier than Max, but Max didn't back down.

"No, Jackson. I'm very curious how you don't think it will hurt you and that pretty little girl you have acting for you," Max said. Jackson nearly punched him.

"Easy," Jackson whispered. "I got home early that night and surprised Emma with flowers. We put the video online. It was a live stream."

Jackson pulled out his phone, swiped the fingerprint scan and scrolled through Facebook.

"See? It got nine-hundred and eighty-seven likes,"

Jackson told Max. He hit play on the video to show Emma walking through the door and seeing a room full of flowers. Her smile lit up the dim garage. She'd been so surprised.

Max grabbed at his phone, obviously looking for the date and time. "I see," he said, his confidence gone for just a split second.

"I sure hope you didn't pay Katy," Jackson needled him, pocketing his phone. "Especially without doing any research. That page is public, by the way."

Max swallowed hard. Jackson was enjoying putting the weasel man in his place. It was almost as good at hitting him. Jackson patted Max's shoulder and continued walking to his car. It was a good thing that Jane had told him to be as public as possible with their relationship.

"There'll just be another girl," Max called out after him. "You'll slip up. It's in your nature."

Jackson turned and smiled at him. "Not with Emma. She's worth it. I'm not giving her up. You're going to be waiting a long time for me to slip. You can go back to being second place in the diaper world."

Max didn't say anything. He just turned and went back out the way they'd come in. Jackson had won.

Jackson waited until he heard the heavy door back to the courtyard slam shut. Even then, he waited for a moment, holding his breath as he walked to his car.

That was a close one. Not because Jackson had done anything wrong, but because Max was a dog with a bone. Max wasn't going to let this go. Max didn't like being second best. He was going to wait for every opportunity to catch Jackson up.

Which wasn't going to happen. Even if his company wasn't on the line, Jackson cared for Emma. She made his stomach twist in the best way and he smiled when she was around. He wasn't going to put her through the emotional torture of having to watch him with another woman.

Even if their relationship was just a contract, he was better than that. He liked her.

No, he decided, **like** *wasn't a strong enough word.*

His mind shied away from what might be a better word. It was a word that he never thought he'd use with a single woman.

Still, he would have to be careful. Max wanted to destroy him. The competition would look for any semblance of infidelity. He would have to be on his guard for women like Katy, trying to get him to agree to drinks.

His phone chimed.

When are you coming home? I'm hungry.

Emma. He couldn't help but smile as he read her text. He quickly typed back that he was just leaving and hurried to his car.

With Emma, he wasn't worried. With her, he wasn't even tempted to return to his old ways. There was no way Max could get anything.

CHAPTER 25

$\mathcal{E}$mma

"I can't believe how good that was," Emma said. She smiled at Jackson. "Thanks for changing our restaurant."

Stars flickered in the night sky as they left the Mexican food restaurant. Emma couldn't believe she'd eaten as much food as she had. Morning sickness hadn't kicked in yet, so food still tasted amazing. She hoped she could keep this good fortune through the rest of her pregnancy.

"It was no problem," Jackson assured her with a smile. "I'm just glad you like Mexican food."

"The tacos were so good," Emma moaned. "The real salsa made the difference. I've only ever had Tex-Mex, and this was so much better."

Jackson grinned at her. "Next time, I'll take you to Mexico. That's the real stuff."

"Really?" Emma asked, pausing as she walked to the car.

"Yes. It's true. The real Mexican food is in Mexico,"

Jackson replied with a laugh. The car unlocked as they approached, the headlights making the parking lot bright.

"No, I mean, going to Mexico," Emma said softly. She shrugged. "I've never been. I've wanted to, but..."

Jackson squeezed her shoulders. "We'll go. Mexico, mountains, islands, wherever you want."

Hope danced across Emma's heart as she imagined a future with Jackson. A real future, not just one where they followed a contract. One where they chose to go to these fabulous places simply to be together.

"Mountains first," she told him. "I think that's what I want to see most. Maybe even some skiing."

Jackson grinned and opened the car door for her. From the corner of her eye, she could see his security team making sure they were safe in the dark parking lot. They were incredibly good at their jobs. She usually forgot they were even there. Now that they were officially engaged, she had her own security team. She was just glad she had gotten the chance to get her pregnancy test without them. They'd been hired the next day.

"Do you have any preference on which mountains?" Jackson asked once she was settled in her seat. He took the driver's seat, which was fine with her. Despite knowing that he could afford hundreds of cars without batting an eyelash, she was still afraid to drive one of these sports cars. If she so much as nicked it, she would feel terrible.

So, she let him drive. Besides, he loved to drive.

"Um..." Emma paused to think. "Big ones. Ones with the tree line thing."

"Tree line thing?" Jackson asked her.

"The mountains that are so tall that trees can't grow any more because of the elevation. Those kinds of mountains," she told him.

"Okay, we can do that," Jackson replied. He looked

thoughtful. "Do you care if it's American, European, or Asian?"

"Nope." She grinned. "Though, I would like to see Mount Everest some day. I don't have any desire to climb it, but I'd like to see it."

"It's beautiful."

"You've been there?" she asked, her voice soft with wonder. She'd never met anyone who had actually been to the world's tallest mountain.

"Yes. I think you'd love it. And the food is amazing."

"I'm glad I'm going to marry you," she blurted out.

He raised an eyebrow and looked over at her. "Is that so?"

"I never would have been able to do any kind of traveling."

"You would have eventually," he replied. "It's not that expensive."

She blushed a little bit. "Plus, I've never had anyone to travel with. That's the other important part. I don't want to go to Everest by myself. I want someone who will enjoy it with me."

His green eyes sparkled in the dark and his mouth curved into the small smile that he only used when he thought she wasn't looking. It was the smile that told her he liked her. Her heart melted.

"I'm excited to show you the world," he murmured, his voice rich in the dark. "There's so much that I want you to see. You're going to light up when I take you to Paris, and you'll love this castle I rent near London."

"We have a future," she said softly. Her hand went to her belly. She hadn't had the appointment yet, but she knew the baby was in there. She wanted to wait until it was a little more official before telling him. She was still so early.

If she told him, he would need to announce it to the world. That was the point of being with him. He would need to use her pregnancy for the benefit of his company. If she miscarried, or was wrong, she didn't want to hurt him. She could only imagine what it would do to his company if he announced a baby only to have it not happen.

So, for now, she was waiting. It made her feel guilty, but she wasn't ready yet. She wasn't sure he was either. For right now, she wanted to focus on making sure that they were good as a couple. This would be the only time they'd have before the baby took over their relationship.

It felt selfish, but the other reason for waiting was so that she could have Jackson all to herself for just a little bit longer. She wanted their relationship to work, and not just because she was with child. She wanted him to enjoy being with her because she was Emma, not just the mother of his child.

"We do have a future," he agreed, flashing her a grin. "A great future."

For a moment, this didn't feel like a contract. This felt like a real date. A real romance. And for just a moment, Emma let herself believe it. She let herself love him without fear. She let herself believe that he would want her, even if he wasn't desperate to save his company.

She loved him.

She knew it was all for show, that there were people watching where they went and what they did, analyzing their relationship from the sidelines, but she still loved him. She couldn't help it. He just made her so happy. He made her feel beautiful and wanted.

He laughed at her jokes. His eyes dilated every time he saw her naked. She felt safe with him. If this wasn't love, then she wasn't sure what else it could be.

Maybe she was just deluding herself into thinking she had feelings for him to make this easier. He obviously liked her, since he didn't have to spend as much time as he did with her. Did that mean that he felt something too? Or was she just pleasant company?

It was so confusing and just made her heart and her head hurt.

"Are you okay?" Jackson asked, coming to a smooth stop at a red light.

"Yeah, why?" she asked, forcing a quick smile.

"You just went quiet all of the sudden," he said. Silence hung between them, heavy and dark in the night. Her heartbeat seemed to stretch into infinity.

"I was just thinking," she said softly. She looked down at the floor of the car. She'd at least gotten used to not worrying about her shoes in the car anymore. Jackson swore she could get the car dirty and he wouldn't mind.

"About what?" he asked. She didn't answer right away, instead waiting for the light to change so he would have to focus on driving. The light stayed red. It had to be the world's longest red light. "You were thinking about the contract," he said, looking up at the light.

She nodded. Her stomach twisted with sudden anxiety. She should just tell him what was on her mind. What was the worst that could happen? He couldn't dump her. He couldn't kick her out.

She took a deep breath. "Yes."

He nodded. His face was strange shadows in the red of the stoplight. He looked up at it, waiting for it to change.

If the light changed, this moment would be gone. He would continue driving and they wouldn't be stuck in this moment anymore.

"I like you," she whispered, afraid that she might break the spell. "I like you a lot."

He glanced over at her and grinned. "I already knew that."

She rolled her eyes. Of course he'd be arrogant and full of himself. "That's not what I'm trying to say, and you know it."

"I know." His eyes didn't leave the light. "I like you a lot, too. Much more than I expected."

"Really?" She was surprised by how much this made her heart race. Her mouth felt dry and sticky.

"Really," he replied. He looked away from the light and over at her. His green eyes filled her soul with bubbling light. "And it's not the contract that has me spending time with you. These dinners aren't in the contract. They're because I want to spend time with you. I'd rather be with you than anyone else."

"Really?" Her voice came out as a squeak.

He smiled. "Really."

He leaned over and kissed her as the light changed. He didn't care that he was supposed to move because he was kissing her. Really kissing her. This wasn't the kiss of a one-night stand or a good time. This was a kiss that meant something.

This was a kiss that lead to love.

When they broke apart, Emma was breathless. She grinned at him and then looked back at the light.

It was red again.

She grinned. That meant she got to kiss him longer this time.

 _mma_

"You must be Emma. It's so wonderful to meet you. You look just like your pictures in the magazines."

Emma stood at the door of Jackson's apartment and suddenly wished very much that she didn't have to do this. But, she didn't really have much of a choice. This had to happen.

"Yes, I'm Emma," she said, forcing herself to smile as she opened the door a little wider. "Please come in. Your name is Becca, right?"

"That's me, Becca the wedding planner," the woman chirped. Becca wasn't much older than Emma, but was several inches shorter. She had beautiful blonde hair in beautiful wavy curls down her back. The woman looked like she just stepped out of a beauty salon.

She wore a light pink dress that looked like 1950's vintage. Her makeup was perfect. Her hair was perfect.

Even though Emma wore nice slacks, a button-up dark blue silk shirt, and light makeup, she felt incredibly unprepared. Becca just looked so put together.

"Now, I have some samples of other weddings so that I can get your opinion on what you want," Becca said, walking through the front door. She pulled two suitcases behind her in matching pink.

"Um, well, Jackson and I were thinking something elegant. I don't want over the top lavish or ornate, but something beautiful," Emma told her. "Here, we can sit at the table here. Would you like some coffee?"

"Oh no, thank you." Becca shook her head. "And, if you want white teeth for the wedding, you shouldn't have coffee either. Or tea. Stick with water. It'll help your figure in your dress, too."

"Oh." Emma wasn't sure what to say to that. She just motioned to the table.

Becca quickly set up shop. She had binders full of pictures and fabric that she laid out systematically on the table.

"You said elegant, correct?" Becca asked, pulling out a specific binder from one of the suitcases. "Take a look in here and tell me what you think."

Emma took the big binder and carefully opened it, unsure of what was going to be inside.

"The first picture is the reception hall of another wedding I did in New York last year," Becca explained. "Everything was seashell cream with bluebird navy accents with a theme of diamonds, because diamonds are forever. Absolutely lovely."

The picture was of a beautiful room decorated into something out of a movie. White and blue were everywhere, along with more glittery gemstones than Emma could count. Everything in the room glittered.

"Wow. Where did you get all the sparkle?" Emma asked,

turning to the next page. It was of a different angle, but still the sparkle remained. "Are they sequins?"

"Those are Swarovski crystals, dear," Becca replied. "Straight from Austria, just for this wedding."

Emma turned the page and found the price tag. She nearly threw up. The crystals were stunning, but not for that price. She could buy several houses for what they paid to make their reception sparkle for just a few hours.

"I think that's a bit much for me," Emma said, setting the binder down. Even though she was marrying a billionaire, she couldn't justify that price.

"Is anyone coming to help you with this?" Becca asked glancing at the door. "Usually there's a mother or a mother in law."

"My mother died a long time ago," Emma replied, ignoring the ache in her chest. "So did Jackson's."

"I see. Is anyone going to help you with these decisions?" Becca asked.

"My matron of honor's little boy has a doctor appointment, but she'll be here once they're done." Emma shrugged. "I was planning on doing most of it myself. I'm not working right now, so I have the time."

Becca looked her over for a moment and then took the binder away. "Let's start from the beginning then. What is your perfect wedding?"

"My perfect wedding? I haven't really thought about it." Emma knew that wasn't true. Her perfect wedding was a private ceremony with only her husband to be, his best man, her maid of honor, and a photographer in a magical spot she'd found in the woods when she was eight. But there was no way that would be appropriate for a billionaire's wedding, especially not one that needed to grab the public's attention.

"Every girl has thought of something," Becca pressed. "Perhaps a castle? A princess like setting?"

Emma shrugged. "Sure. That'll work."

"Emma, I don't want what will work. I want to know what you're dreaming of," Becca said, taking Emma's hands in hers. "This is supposed to be your big day. It should be what you want it to be. Surely you thought of what you would look like walking down the aisle with your father in a beautiful dress?"

The image of her father's face hit Emma like a slap. He wouldn't walk her down the aisle. He wouldn't give her away. Her mother wouldn't dab at her eyes with a Kleenex. They would never see Emma married. Even if it was just a sham marriage.

Emma broke down in tears as Becca looked at her baffled.

"Excuse me for a moment." Emma quickly stood from the table and ran to the bedroom. She closed the door behind her and sank onto the foot of the bed. There, she sobbed. Tears ran down her face as she tried to keep her gasps and cries low enough that Becca wouldn't come in and bother her. She wasn't sure where this sudden outpour of emotion was coming from, but if she didn't release it, she would explode.

What would Mama think of this? Emma thought, tears streaming down her face. Would she be proud of me for marrying a billionaire? Would Daddy like Jackson? Or would he be gruff and always be cleaning a shotgun when Jackson came over?

Emma wasn't sure. She thought her mother would like Jackson, but she wasn't sure if her mother would approve of the reasons for their marriage.

Granted, even if she was alive, her mother wouldn't know the real reason for their marriage.

Emma sighed and wiped at her cheeks. She would never know what her parents would think of this. The best she could do was imagine they were happy because she was going to be happy. She took a deep breath and went back out to the kitchen.

"Sorry about that," Emma said, settling back into her chair.

Becca shrugged. "It happens more than you might think," she said kindly. "Weddings are stressful things. Emotions, family, obligations, and guests all make things difficult. That's why I'm here. I'm here to help."

"Okay." Emma gave the other woman a weak smile. "I'm going to need a lot of help."

"That's why I'm the best. Let's start simple. Big or small wedding?"

"Go big or go home, right?" Emma supplied.

"It's what you want," Becca told her. "You aren't limited by funds, so you can have a big wedding."

Emma wished Jackson were here. She wasn't sure what he wanted other than, "make it big and impressive. Whatever you want as long as we have the public's attention for the day." She was going to have him come to the next one of these meetings.

"How about time?" Becca asked, shifting away to a different approach. "You said as soon as possible. It's summer now, so I would suggest, if you really want the very best, to wait and have a winter wedding. With your dark hair, it would be stunning."

"A winter wedding?" Emma thought about it. Snow falling as she kissed Jackson. It would be beautiful. Except, she was pregnant. If she did her math right, this baby was coming early spring. For a winter wedding, she'd be as big as a house.

Suddenly the image in her head changed to her ridiculously pregnant as they kissed in the snow. She didn't want that either.

"No, on the winter wedding," Emma quickly said. "I want a summer wedding. This summer."

"This summer?" Becca's eyes widened. She picked up one of the binders and flipped through it. "The best places are already booked..."

"This summer," Emma repeated. "I want it as soon as possible. I don't care what it costs."

"Okay. It's your wedding," Becca replied. Emma could see the dollar signs going off in her head. "Like I said, I'm here to help. Anything you need."

"You know what?" An idea came to Emma. "I want you to plan it all. Plan a wedding fit for a billionaire. Jackson has given you the budget. Make it work. If you need more funds to take care of more, let me know."

The idea of Becca taking care of everything relieved a huge weight from Emma's shoulders she didn't realize she was carrying. She'd thought she was looking forward to planning the wedding, but now that Becca was here, it was the last thing in the world Emma wanted to worry about.

"Are you sure?" Becca looked surprised.

"Positive," Emma assured her. "I just want to pick out my dress. Everything else, is yours. The invitations, the decorations, the location. All of it. As long as it's done by Fall, and it's something that will look good in a magazine, I'm happy."

"Well, this isn't how I normally do things," Becca said slowly, a smile filling her face. "But I can do it. How about I give you three options tomorrow? You pick your favorite, and I'll do the rest."

"That sounds perfect," Emma agreed.

"Okay. I'm going to go work on the proposals for you." Becca rose from the table. "You're sure this is what you want to do?"

"One of the perks of marrying a billionaire is that you can

pay people to do just about everything," Emma told her. "So, I'm going to pay you to do just about everything."

"You won't regret it," Becca promised. "This wedding will be a dream wedding. People will talk about it for years. It'll be perfect."

"Then I'm happy," Emma told her. If everyone were talking about it, then Jackson would be happy too. Maybe someday Emma could convince Jackson to have the small, intimate ceremony Emma had dreamed of. That one she could plan.

Becca quickly picked up her things and stuffed them into her suitcases. The woman was beaming with excitement. She was going to plan the multi-million dollar wedding of her dreams. Becca had every right to be excited.

"I will see you tomorrow at ten," Becca announced, heading out the door. She was practically skipping with excitement.

"See you tomorrow," Emma said, offering a wave.

Becca disappeared out the door and Emma finally let herself relax. She slumped into her chair and noticed a bridal magazine Becca had dropped. Emma picked it up and thumbed through it, looking at the checklists and details.

She smiled and set the magazine on the table. She didn't have to deal with any of it. This wedding planning stuff was going to be easier than she thought.

CHAPTER 27

Jackson woke feeling more rested than he had in months. He lay in bed for a moment, his eyes closed and body still, enjoying the lack of exhaustion. He wasn't sure what had woken him, but it wasn't his alarm. It wasn't a need to move or a desire to get the day started.

It was that he just wasn't tired anymore.

He peeked open one eye to see the world bathed in sunlight. It was strange that he'd slept so late. Usually, he was up and running by dawn. There was too much for him to do in the world to lay around sleeping all day.

Yet, he had relaxed today. He looked over to see Emma curled up beside him. Her chest rose and fell with easy, deep breaths that told him she was still fast asleep. He smiled, watching her for a moment.

When she was here, he felt at peace. There was no need to

push for the next thing. He still wanted to excel, of course, but the need for better stopped when she was around. She was the best. He was content.

It was a strange feeling. Usually, when he woke up with a woman in his bed, he couldn't wait to be rid of her. He didn't let many women stay the night for precisely that reason. He always woke up the next morning disappointed and ready to search for the next one.

The women he was used to satisfied him for a night, maybe two.

But not Emma. Emma made his world come into focus. When she smiled, he didn't feel the need to look elsewhere for more. She was enough for him.

She was more than enough.

He carefully brushed a dark strand of hair from her cheek. She sighed in her sleep, but didn't wake. He thought of kissing her, waking her gently with erotic touches and making the morning start out right.

The low heat in his belly and the growing erection told him it was the right thing to do, but his heart said to let her sleep. She looked so peaceful, so content, that he didn't want to take that away from her just to satisfy his own needs.

Not that she wouldn't enjoy it. She always amazed him with her energy and desire. She wanted him as much as he wanted her. There was no fake orgasms or false cries of delight. She meant every sound, every groan of pleasure.

He was a lucky man.

She sighed again and rolled over in her sleep, pulling the covers around her shoulders in the process. Jackson found himself without a sheet.

She was a heavenly creature, except she did like to steal the covers.

He chuckled softly and carefully got out of bed. He tiptoed to the closet, grabbed a soft robe, and then left her to sleep. He would pleasure her later. It was more fun if she was awake anyway.

He padded to the kitchen, feeling happy despite the fact that all he had done today was woken up. That was Emma's doing as well. Just being around her made him happy. He thought again of waking her, satisfying both his need and hers, but poured a cup of coffee instead.

Waiting would make it all the sweeter later. It was like waiting for Christmas. If he was patient, it would be so much better than opening his presents early. An awake Emma, making those soft moans that he loved so much was worth it.

He took his coffee and phone and sat down on the couch. Sunshine filled the room. He had no idea that the view was so nice in the morning from his apartment. He was used to being out and to the office by dawn most days that he didn't sit and appreciate it.

He checked his emails, checked the news, and checked his investments. Everything was doing well and that was do to Emma. She had won the hearts of the mothers that bought his products. And the fact that she was so saccharine sweet made him sweet by association.

And that was just fine by him.

He sighed and checked his watch. It was still early and he wanted to let her sleep. He glanced at the table and saw a wedding magazine. She'd told him that she was giving the wedding planner and Jane free rein to make the wedding the perfect.

He knew she preferred a small ceremony, but that she was going to give him the big, elaborate wedding he wanted. She was willing to give up her dream wedding to give him, and his company, what they needed. He didn't know many women who would be willing to do that.

How had he found someone that was so willing to work

with him and give him exactly what he needed? Not just in the bedroom, but in daily life and in business?

He loved her.

The thought came out of nowhere. It was a good thing he was sitting down because he felt a little lightheaded just thinking it.

Yet, it rang with truth. Just thinking the words made his body tighten and relax at the same time. He'd never felt anything like this for anyone in his life. He knew without a doubt that he would die for her. He would do anything to make her happy.

He would give up his company to be with her. If the board of directors came to him and told him that it was her or his position, he would give up his job in a heartbeat. He wouldn't even think twice.

He loved her.

Jackson leaned back against the couch, breathless with his revelation. He wanted to run into the bedroom and tell her. He wanted to shout it from the rooftops and post it on every social media outlet there was. He seriously considered hiring a sky-writing plane just because the world would know that he loved her.

But all those things were just show. He wanted to do something more. He wanted to give her something.

Jewelry? She didn't wear much. It wasn't important to her. She would ooh and ahh over it, but it wouldn't mean anything special.

He'd already given her a flower-shop of roses. She'd loved them, but it wasn't what he was looking for.

A food? A car? A lion with a golden leash?

What would make her smile and know that he cared? He sighed, racking his brain and looking around the apartment for inspiration. His eyes settled on the picture of mountains.

She wanted to see mountains.

He picked up his phone and started making plans. It couldn't be this week as he couldn't get out of business obligations, but he could take her in two weeks. The Swiss Alps would be perfect. He knew a little place that they could share a magical time.

This would be a wonderful surprise. He didn't want to tell her just yet. He would whisk her away on a private jet and have her open her eyes to the surprise of a lifetime. It was the perfect gift.

He could already see her smile in his mind as he sent emails to his secretary to start booking things. He smiled as he added a small wedding ceremony to the itinerary. It would be just for the two of them. A mountain wedding of her dreams. The one she actually wanted.

They could still have the big one later, and the press could have all the pictures they wanted, but he would give her the private ceremony on top of a mountain that she wanted. That she deserved. Something for just the two of them.

A real wedding. He wanted a real wedding, because he loved her. And this relationship was no longer about the contract and business anymore.

 ackson

Jackson heard the door to the bedroom open and the soft footsteps of Emma as she emerged from the bedroom. It wasn't a moment too soon. He'd just finished on the phone setting up the site for his surprise wedding to Emma. He felt giddy with excitement.

"I can't believe I slept so late," Emma mumbled, stumbling out into the sunshine. "Did you sleep as well as I did?"

"Better," he assured her.

She came over and kissed the top of his head. "You never stop working, do you?" she asked, motioning to the phone in his hands.

"I didn't wake you, did I?" He hoped she hadn't heard him talking on the phone.

She shook her head. "No. My need for coffee woke me."

She squeezed his shoulder and walked to the kitchen to pour herself a cup of coffee.

Jackson let out a small sigh of relief. The surprise wasn't ruined. She thought he was working, not planning a magical vacation. He smiled, pleased with his surprise.

"You look far too happy this morning," Emma said, joining him on the couch. He loved the way she curled her feet up under her as she sat next to him.

"Things are good in my world," he told her with a smile. "Very good."

"Business is picking up then?" Emma asked, taking a small sip of coffee. She grimaced and set it down on the coffee table.

"Yes, business is fine," he replied. "Is something wrong with your coffee?"

"I think the milk spoiled," she said, shaking her head. "It doesn't taste right."

He frowned. It wasn't like the his staff to purchase or keep spoiled milk in the house. "I'll have someone get new milk today."

"Did your coffee taste funny?" she asked, looking at his empty cup on the table. "It could be the coffee."

"My coffee was fine." His frown deepened. "Let me taste yours."

He picked up the cup and took a sip. It tasted fine, if maybe a little sweet for his preference. There didn't seem to be any problem with the milk or the coffee.

"I don't taste anything," he said, slowly setting the cup down. "Are you sure?"

Emma swallowed hard. "It must just be a weird day."

Jackson turned and looked her over. She looked exhausted, even though he knew she'd slept all night. Dark circles hung under her beautiful eyes. She sat with her legs tucked carefully under her, and her dark hair was messy in her ponytail.

A moment of possessive concern washed over him. He needed to make sure she was okay. He needed to protect her from whatever was making her look this tired. He would fight a dragon with a sword if that was what it would take, but he was going to protect her.

"Are you feeling okay?" he asked, keeping quiet about the desire to battle dragons for her. He reached over and smoothed a stray strand of hair from her face. She gave him a weak smile.

"Yeah..." She paused and took a deep breath. "Actually, there's something I need to talk to you about."

"You can tell me anything," he said immediately. He meant it too. Short of her telling him she was in love with someone else, there was nothing he couldn't hear from her.

"I had this big plan, but..." She looked up at him, a hint of fear in her eyes. "I should just do it now."

"Like I said, you can tell me anything." He gave her a confident smile, even though his insides were twisting. He could already imagine half a dozen absolutely terrible things and another half that were only mostly terrible.

But he didn't show it. He kept his face calm and his body serene. It was his secret to business. Never let 'em see you sweat.

Emma took a deep breath. "Jackson, I'm..." She opened and closed her mouth twice. "You know what? It'll be easier if I just show you."

She got up from the couch, swaying slightly as she stood. She gave him a shrug and hurried to her purse on the counter. He watched her, memorizing everything that he could. He didn't know what she had to show him, but if she was this nervous, it couldn't be good.

She clutched a small piece of paper. It looked shiny, like a photograph. He wondered what she could possibly have. Photos in his world, though, were rarely a good thing. They were usually for blackmail or divorce settlements.

She stood before him, her breath coming in shallow pants. She chewed on her lip and every inch of her body said she was nervous.

"I had this really amazing plan to make you dinner, and make this special," she said. He was having a hard time focusing on her words he was staring at the paper in her hands so hard. "But, I want you to know. You deserve to know."

She swallowed hard and took a deep breath before handing him the picture.

He took the paper like it might bite him. It looked to be upside down, but when he turned it over it still didn't make sense. The photo was black with a tiny gray smudge to the right. He frowned trying to figure out what she was telling him with this. He was going to be sucked down a black hole? She was going to bury him in a place so dark no one would ever find him?

"You're going to be a father." Her voice was small and far away.

Slowly, it dawned on him what he was looking at. This was an ultrasound of a pregnancy. Emma was pregnant. This was their baby. The photo in his hands, this strange, grainy, picture of space, was the first picture of his child. Their child.

"You're... you're..." Jackson's mouth and tongue couldn't seem to form the words. His entire life, he'd tried *not* to get the women he slept with pregnant. He was always careful and never let his guard down.

He hadn't thought it would be so quick with Emma. He knew couples who tried for years before seeing success. They'd barely been together over a month, and here was the result of their passion.

"Yes, Jackson," Emma said. She was watching him, waiting to see his reaction. "I'm pregnant with your child."

He looked down at the picture again. He was a father.

"What are you thinking, Jackson?" Emma asked. He looked up to see her biting her lip and looking like she was about to cry. "Please, tell me what you're thinking."

"I'm thinking you are the most beautiful woman in the entire world," he told her. He stood up and put his arms around her. She was shaking. "I'm thinking that I am the luckiest man in the world."

A shudder of relief went through her and she collapsed into him, tucking her face into his shoulder. He rubbed her back.

"I was so afraid..." Her words came out muffled, but he understood them.

"Why?" he asked, pulling her back.

She shrugged. "I don't know. Your reputation?"

"It's in our contract."

"Yeah, but so are sales taxes and membership fees. Just because it's in a contract doesn't mean that it's something you want," she replied.

He took her chin in his hand, making sure that she looked up at him. She was so beautiful it made his heart catch. If he had felt protective before, this was a thousand times more.

"I want this," he told her, his voice going low. "I want you. I want this."

With his other hand he touched her belly. She sniffled and fell into him again. He wrapped his arms around her, letting her sniffle and relax against him.

They stood there, him comforting her and contemplating his future. The idea of a child that was now a real thing was overwhelming. It was a good kind of overwhelming, but still more than he had expected. They'd both known this was coming, but he thought they'd have more time.

His heart thudded in his chest. He was going to be a father. The only word he could think to describe the feeling taking over him was joy. He was going to be a father.

For this moment, he didn't care that it would help his company. He wasn't thinking about that.

He was thinking of bike lessons and piano lessons. How to treat a skinned knee, and where they were going to put the nursery. Would it be a boy or a girl? Would they want to go into the family business or do something else? Would they be an artist or an astronaut?

He didn't know, but he couldn't wait to find out. How in the world was he going to wait 9 months to meet this little person that he already adored?

Not to mention Emma. He wanted to make sure she had the best of everything. The best doctors, the best hospitals, the best food, the best everything. He would make sure this was the best pregnancy that money could buy.

He wanted her to be as happy as he was.

At least, they could still go to the mountains. He would cancel the ski trip and the more adventurous activities, but they could still enjoy the beautiful sights and the amazing food. He would just make sure to have a doctor on staff as well.

"You okay?" he asked, rubbing her back. He wasn't sure how long they'd been standing there, but it felt like a long time. That one small sentence, *I'm pregnant*, still had him spinning. It didn't feel real yet.

She sniffled and pulled back, but this time she was smiling. "Yeah. I am." She looked up at him with those big eyes. "Are you?"

"I'm fantastic," he assured her. He grinned. "Absolutely fantastic."

She grinned at him and her old happy spark came back to her face.

"There is a small problem that you should know about, though," she said, trying to keep a straight face and failing.

"What?" he asked, unsure of where she was headed with this.

"I'm not going to fit in a wedding dress for very long," she said, giving him a sly grin. He laughed.

"It's a good thing I didn't want to wait then, isn't it?" He leaned over and kissed her forehead. He was going to marry her next week. Who cared about the dress when he felt this happy?

ackson

He was going to be a father.

As he kissed Emma, knowing that he was going to marry this woman in just a couple short weeks, he felt happy.

Not just happy. Joy. Pure joy.

He was in love with the most beautiful woman on the planet, she loved him, and she was carrying their child. He didn't know that it was possible to have a heart this full and not have it burst. He felt like he could fly his chest was so full of light.

He was going to be a father.

He kissed her, wanting her to know just how much he cared. Jackson was good with words in the boardroom and when negotiating, but when it came to emotions, he didn't know what to say. It had never mattered before now.

He'd never cared for another person like this.

So, instead of words he kissed her. He let his tongue show her instead of speaking.

It started out as a sweet kiss. It started out pure and wonderful. And then it grew from there. Lust colored the edges of their kiss, slowly creeping in and making things deeper. He wanted more than just to kiss her.

She pulled back, her eyes big and dark. Her soul was there, watching him. She smiled and flushed.

"You are so beautiful," he told her. He meant it. In that moment, he couldn't think of another woman that he found more lovely than her. She was perfect in his eyes.

"You're not so bad yourself," she teased, her voice husky. She bit her lower lip, and grinned at him in an obvious invitation for more.

"Come with me," he said, standing from the couch and taking her hand. She followed him willingly to the bedroom, where he shut the door, keeping the lights low. Summer sunshine still brightened everything, but it was cool and comfortable in here.

He took her to the bed. From there, he carefully pulled her over-sized shirt up and over her head. She giggled as he tossed it to the floor. He was glad to see she didn't cover herself, despite the fact that the sunshine made her skin glow.

She wasn't embarrassed in front of him anymore. It made his heart happy.

He knelt before her, tugging on her cotton panties until they fell around her ankles. She giggled as he kissed the spot just below her bellybutton. Their child was growing in there. The little baby was going to be beautiful like its mother. It didn't matter if it was a boy or a girl, Jackson loved it with all his heart already.

"Lay down," he commanded, his voice soft. She smiled as she crawled into the big bed. Her dark hair spilled across the pillow and her eyes followed his every movement. He stripped for her, making sure to give her a little bit of a show in the process.

He loved her low giggle and the way she rubbed her legs together as she watched him. He'd never worried about his appearance, but knowing that she found him attractive was addictive.

He started at her feet, kissing each toe and up to her ankles. Every inch of her skin was worth worshiping. He lavished kisses, loving on her soft skin as he made his way up her calves, kissing each knee, and onto her thighs. She stilled as he kissed her hip bones, holding still for him.

He could smell her desire, but he wasn't going to stop his kisses there.

He kissed her belly, her ribs, her breasts. She hummed with pleasure as he kissed the spot between her shoulder and neck. He kissed her arms down to the palms of her hands. She was so beautiful he was sure he would run out of kisses before he could match her beauty to them.

"Jackson," Emma whispered. She reached out and put her hand to his cheek. She didn't need to say more. He could see it in her eyes what she wanted.

She wanted him.

Carefully, he positioned himself over her. She looked up at him with complete adoration as he nudged her legs just a little bit wider. He was hard now. It was impossible not to be hard while he kissed her body.

The low ache in his belly told him just how badly he wanted her. It didn't matter that she already carried his child. He wanted to fill her with his seed again and again and again. He wanted to make sure that every creature on the planet knew that she was his.

It was primal.

He paused at her entrance, looking into her eyes. She bit

her lip as he pushed upward. The gasp of pleasure shivered over him as he entered her. He loved the way her eyes darkened and then rolled into the back of her head as he made her his.

Every inch of him was warm now. Warm and secure. He almost hated to pull out, but he did so knowing that he could dive into her depths again if he did. The way her body tightened around him, drawing him in was something that never got old.

He went slow, enjoying every sensation. His hands were on either side of his head as he worked his hips in tandem with hers. She moaned, low and deep as he made love to her. He took his right hand and brushed away a strand of dark hair from her face and she turned, pressing her cheek into his palm.

This was making love, he realized. This wasn't sex or fucking. This was love. This was why sex was called making love. Every thrust of his hips was a way to connect to her. A physical connection of their two bodies, joining to form a new soul.

This was what he had been missing all this time. Sure, fucking was amazing, and he still wanted to fuck Emma's brains out, but this was different. This was better.

This was love.

His heart ached with the knowledge. He loved her. He loved their life and their future together. This was what all the storybooks meant. This was how Prince Charming ended up being happily ever after with only princess.

"Jackson," Emma whispered, calling out his name as she arched her back. She was close to orgasm, close to falling off the edge of pleasure that he created.

He pushed harder, giving her the last bit to crest the edge. Her face stilled and her eyes closed into concentration as she came hard on him.

Her internal muscles rolled over him, pulling him inside of her and begging him to come with her. He closed his eyes and followed her into oblivion, letting his body join the ecstasy of his heart. For a single moment, time stood still and all he knew was joy.

The moment ended, but only the physical overwhelming sensation. The love was still there. Emma opened her eyes and looked up at him. He was all she saw as she smiled and cupped his cheek in her hand.

He rolled over and she snuggled into the nook of his arm. Pure contentment washed over him. In this moment, he'd never been happier. He couldn't imagine feeling happier. It just wasn't possible. This was more than he could have ever asked for. It was more than he deserved.

"I love you," Emma whispered, tucking her head into his shoulder. She looked up at him and smiled, her dark eyes sparkling.

He wanted to say the words back. He certainly felt them. But his mouth wouldn't make the motions. He had spent too many years denying the fact that he was even capable of love. He was a player. Players didn't love.

So he didn't say anything. He kissed her forehead and felt guilt creep into his happiness.

Emma sighed softly, but didn't pull away. Instead she snuggled into him further, her breath coming slower and deeper.

She was almost asleep in his arms. He didn't dare move. He still wished he could say the words. He wanted to.

"I love you," she murmured, her voice drifting into sleep. She sighed and stilled in his arms and he knew she was dreaming.

He tried to mouth the words, but even that was too hard. He loved her. He knew it in the depths of his soul, but yet, saying the words wasn't happening.

He sighed. She would be patient with him, he knew that. She deserved to know how much she meant to him though. She deserved to hear him say it.

In the mountains, he decided. *I'll tell her then. I'll call it out to the world. It has to be special. I have to make it perfect so she always knows that I love her.*

Content now with his decision, he sighed and held her to him. He didn't sleep, but instead planned of their future and how he would tell her he loved her in a way she would never forget.

ackson

"I don't have to go," Jackson told the beautiful woman laying in bed.

Emma rolled over and hugged the bowl closer to her chest.

"And what are you going to do if you stay here? Sit and watch me throw up?" she asked, motioning to the bowl.

Morning sickness had hit her hard. He'd been surprised to learn that it really should be called All Day sickness as it didn't occur just in the morning. It actually seemed to be worse for Emma right before bed.

"I don't like leaving you," he said, softly. He sat on the edge of the bed and caressed her hair. She hummed slightly, leaning into him.

"I'll be fine," she promised. "Honestly, I just want to lay in bed, drink the ginger tea you got me, and watch horrible, trashy TV. There's a new episode."

Jackson rolled his eyes and then narrowed them. "You aren't hyping the morning sickness so you can stay home and watch the new episode are you?"

"Me?" Emma's eyes got big and innocent as she held up a hand to her chest. "I would never."

"You so would," he accused.

She smiled. "Possibly," she admitted. Then she froze and turned a little green. The playfulness went out of her eyes and she reached for the bowl.

"You okay?" Jackson asked. He knew that it was just the baby hormones, but he still hated to see her like this.

She took a deep breath and let it out slowly. "Yeah. Just got too confident." She smiled up at him. "Go to the party. Have fun. I'll be more comfortable here. Besides, I've been looking forward to this show all week."

"Seriously?" he asked. The show was garbage. He couldn't understand what she saw it in. No sane person would want to watch it unless they were being tortured.

"Yes. It's my guilty pleasure," she replied. "You are welcome to make fun of me for it, but I am watching it and enjoying every trashy, mascara-streaked moment."

He didn't rise from the bed. It felt like he was cheating on her. He was off to an amazing dinner party with wine, food, and entertainment while she was stuck here in bed puking her guts out.

"Go," she said, giving him a gentle push. "My show comes on in five minutes and I know you hate it. If you're still here, not only will you miss out on your party, but you will have to watch my show."

He shivered. Reality television was like nails on a chalkboard for Jackson. He would literally rather stare at a blank screen for an hour than listen to people whine about their made-for-TV love lives.

"You're sure?" he asked, one more time. He stood up slowly. "I'll stay and we can watch action movies?"

"I'm watching this in three minutes," she told him. She took the remote and tucked it under her pillow. "You're going to go have a nice time. If you don't leave soon, you're going to be late."

"I'll be home soon," he promised, giving her one last kiss on the forehead.

She looked up at him, her eyes soft and full of love. "You look nice in the new suit," she told him. "You're going to break all the girls' hearts."

"As long as it's not yours. I'll break them all and come home to you."

She smiled, her eyes stealing his breath with the amount of love in them. His heart forgot how to beat it was so full for a moment. The protective instinct nearly overwhelmed him, but he knew if he stayed he would regret it. He had been looking forward to this dinner party probably as much as she had been looking forward to her new show.

She looked up as he reached the bedroom door and waved to him, still clutching the bowl like it was the only thing keeping her upright in bed. She smiled and blew him a kiss before going back to the TV. The intro music started and he darted out before he had to suffer through a second of the show.

Jackson enjoyed the party immensely. He wished that Emma could be there, but even without her, he was enjoying himself. The food and drink were delicious and he'd found a college friend he hadn't seen in years. He'd spent the majority of the evening catching up and reminiscing.

The best part to him, was that despite remembering the "good old days" with a different girl every night, he had no desire to repeat them. He was glad that he got to go home to Emma at the end of the night tonight.

It took the pressure off. He was no longer hunting the crowd for the best girl to bring home. He wasn't distracted by previous conquests, and no jealous husbands threatened to punch his lights out. Jackson was sure that his security team appreciated the change of pace as well.

Jackson stepped outside onto a porch overlooking the water. The party was held at the yacht club clubhouse, so the view was amazing. The second story porch jutted out over the docks where million dollar boats bobbed in the cool night air.

Most everyone was inside enjoying the party, but Jackson wanted a moment to himself to check in with Emma. He could see her Facebook status was active, so he knew she was awake.

"How's your show?" he asked when she picked up the phone.

"The new guy is a total jerk, and I hate him," she replied.

"Maybe he'll get voted off next week," he consoled.

"What? No! That would be terrible," she replied. "I like that I hate him. It makes the show so much more interesting."

"So you're enjoying watching a show full of people you hate?"

"Yes, but only because I know they aren't real people," she replied. "It's like getting to gossip without hurting anyone. I get my fix of crazy without actually interacting with the crazy."

"You know that makes absolutely no sense, right?" He

shook his head and looked out at the dark water. Some of the docked yachts had people sitting out on the decks enjoying drinks and having conversations.

"Forty million people can't be wrong," Emma replied. He could hear her smile over the phone.

He sighed and shook his head. This was something he was going to have to live with. His future wife enjoyed horrible television. He smiled, knowing it could be so, so much worse.

"So, how's the party?" Emma asked. He heard the TV lower in the background.

"It's wonderful," he told her. "I'm glad I came. I ran into an old friend and I have some wine for you to try later."

"I can't have wine for awhile," she reminded him. "But thank you anyway."

His heart skipped a beat. He was still coming to terms with the fact that she was pregnant. So much was going to change.

"Right. Next year then," he said. "You feeling better?"

"The tea is helping. But laying down is helping the most."

"How long is this supposed to last again?" he asked, leaning against the porch railing. "I'm having a good time, but I'd be having more fun if you were here."

"According to the doctor, the nausea should stop in the second trimester. So, I have two more months of this crap. But, I should be good for all the Christmas parties, at least."

"Then I will make sure you go to all of them." He heard the TV volume go up at little bit and realized she was still trying to watch her show. He should go back to the party anyway. "I'm going to be home in a few hours."

"Okay. Wake me up when you get back. I..." She paused, stopping her words from coming out. He knew she was going to say, "I love you," but since he hadn't said it back yet, she didn't want to pressure him.

He wanted to make it special. She deserved to feel like a princess when he said it. He wanted her to never doubt it and the only way he knew how to make that happen was to make it an amazing event. The trip to the mountains would do it.

He would just love her without saying the words and screwing everything up until then.

"I'll see you soon," she said. "Have a great night. I love you."

"You too," he replied warmly. He clicked off the phone and looked down at her picture on his screen. He smiled at her image. "I love you."

He sighed and looked out at the water again. He could hear murmurs of conversation on the various yachts and soft sounds of music and conversation from inside the club house. The stars shone down on the porch, twinkling in the darkness.

"I'm so sorry to bother you," a soft feminine voice said from behind him. "But, are you Jackson Weathers?"

Jackson turned to see a young woman in a stunning red dress. It fit her every curve, hinting at smooth skin underneath. It was sexy without being slutty. He wondered immediately where he could get Emma a dress just like it.

"I am," he replied, tucking his phone into his pocket.

"Oh my gosh." She grinned and looked like she might bounce off the porch with excitement. "I was so hoping you'd be here tonight. I've wanted to meet you forever."

Jackson smiled at her. It was always nice to meet a fan. "And you are?"

"Alexa," she replied, grinning and tucking a perfect golden curl behind her ear. She reached out her hand. "I'm a business student at the local college, and you are such an inspiration."

He shook her hand firmly, noticing the way her cheeks

flushed at his touch. Two months ago, he would have been figuring out if he wanted to take her to his apartment or a hotel bed. She was beautiful and obviously attracted to him. He knew that all he had to do was smile and she would do whatever he wanted.

Except he didn't want her. Alexa was beautiful and obviously attracted to him, but he didn't want to take her to any of his beds.

He released her hand. "It's very nice to meet you, Alexa," he told her. She held onto his hand for an extra moment.

"Could I ask you a couple of questions?" She smiled up at him. "Like I said, I'm a business student. I was wondering if you could give me a couple of tips."

She bit her bottom lip as she looked up at him. When Emma did it, he wanted to kiss her. When Alexa did it, he wanted to tell her it looked childish and was smearing the red of her lipstick.

"Maybe some other time," he said. "I was actually just on my way out."

"You're leaving?" She glanced out at the yachts behind him. "But it's such a nice night. And isn't one of those yachts yours?"

She tugged gently at his arm, turning him to look out at the water with her. She stood far too close for comfort. This used to happen all the time and he would let it happen. He wasn't used to having to tell women no.

"I'm very sorry, Alexa," he said, gently pulling his arm away from her. "But it's time for me to leave."

She frowned slightly and then moved forward, wrapping her arm around his neck and kissing him. The shock of it had him frozen for a second before he quickly pushed her off.

"What the fuck are you doing?" He spat, stepping away from her.

"I thought that's how you liked it," Alexa replied, batting her eyelashes and doing the annoying lip-bite. "They say that women who sleep with you are more likely to get a job at your company. Isn't this how this works?"

"Not even a little bit," he said.

Jackson stared at her for a second before leaving the porch. He walked past her, carefully not touching her as he went back into the party.

He couldn't believe the woman had kissed him like that. He hadn't seen it coming at all. Something about it made him feel sick to his stomach, and it wasn't just that he'd been kissed by a stranger.

He thought of other encounters that had started just like that and played out differently. Alexa wasn't wrong. He'd slept with several women who had become employees. If they wanted to sleep their way to the top, he wasn't going to stop them. He just wasn't going to promote them if they weren't good at their jobs either.

He'd had hundreds of encounters just like this one that had led to one-night stands he never regretted. Yet, this made his stomach turn.

This felt like a set-up. It was too easy. He thought of the people down on the yachts. It would be far too easy for one of them to have a camera and to have gotten a picture of their kiss. Without context, it would have looked consensual.

"Shit," he hissed. What if this wasn't just an attempt to sleep with the big boss? What if this was something else?

And worse, how would he explain it to Emma?

He wouldn't. He wouldn't tell her. He didn't need to worry her, he decided. His stomach twisted and a small voice told him it was a bad idea.

He didn't want to tell the beautiful woman pregnant with his child that his lips had been touched by someone else. He was embarrassed. She deserved better than him.

He didn't want to tell a soul.

He left the party. He was no longer in the mood.

CHAPTER 31

Emma groaned, finally giving up on her nap. Exhaustion still tugged on her, but her phone simply wouldn't stop buzzing or chiming. Unfortunately, it was on the kitchen table and a good ten steps away from the couch she currently was very comfortable on.

The chime went off again. She thought about just leaving it there, but it was plugged in. The chimes would never stop since it would never run out of battery. Besides, that many text messages, emails, and phone calls had to be something important.

With a groan, she threw her feet to the floor and sat up from the couch. She just wanted to nap today. This being pregnant thing was harder than she expected. She remembered her friend Grace's pregnancy being easy. The only thing Grace had was an aversion to the smell of cooked chicken. Emma seemed to have an aversion to everything.

She stood up and walked zombie like to the kitchen table. She picked up her phone and started making some ginger tea while she checked what was making her phone so noisy.

Twenty-two text messages, but only three of them from numbers she recognized.

Sixty-eight emails. Twenty-three phone calls, all with voicemail messages.

Emma raised an eyebrow in confusion as she looked at her phone. Where in the world had all these people gotten her contact information? Jackson had assured her that this was a private line when he gave it to her. No one was supposed to know it, yet there were twenty-three phone calls stating otherwise.

She went to open up the text messages when the phone began to vibrate again. She nearly dropped it she was so startled. No one ever called her. She decided to answer it and find out who exactly wanted to get her attention.

"Hello?"

"Hello? Ms. Sheridan? Ms. Emma Sheridan?" A female voice on the other line asked, sounding slightly surprised.

"Yes, that's me. How can I help you?"

"I'm with the Daily Times and was hoping you could give me a comment," the voice replied. She sounded nice enough.

"A comment about what?" Emma asked. "And how did you get this number?"

"A comment about the photo of Jackson Weathers kissing another woman," the reporter replied. "Just days after proposing."

A cold chill settled into Emma's stomach.

"No comment," Emma quickly said. "Do not call back."

She quickly hung up. She closed her eyes. Maybe this was an old photo. Maybe it was a misunderstanding.

She pulled up the internet and ran a quick search.

The very first article had a picture of Jackson kissing a

beautiful blonde woman. Her arms were wrapped around him in a passionate embrace. She was absolutely gorgeous and everything that Jackson usually went for.

In other words, not plain-Jane Emma.

"Maybe it's an old picture they're trying to pass off as new," she mumbled. She tapped on the picture, even though it made her stomach flip. Seeing one's fiancé kissing another tended to have that reaction.

Emma's heart stuttered and her knees gave out. She reached for a kitchen chair and collapsed into it, staring at the photo.

He was wearing his blue suit. His *new* blue suit. She could see him putting it on while she lay in bed.

Had he worn it knowing he was going to meet her? Had he wanted to impress this new lover? She tried to think back to exactly what had happened two nights ago. She'd been sick and wanted to stay home. She had watched her favorite reality TV show.

She had thought it had been her decision not to go to the party, but now she wasn't so sure. Maybe he had played her. He was known to be a player.

She swallowed hard and read the article. Maybe it was just a bad angle... maybe...

"'Jackson Weathers kissed me,' Alexa J. told reporters this morning. 'He instigated it. He offered to take me to his yacht, but I didn't want to leave the party yet. I was there to make business contacts, so when the biggest billionaire in the city offered to show me the ropes, I jumped on the opportunity to speak to him alone.'"

Emma read the article, her heart breaking with every word. Jackson had found a beautiful woman.

"'I thought we were alone,' Alexa J. says. 'I knew he was seeing someone, but I thought it was serious. I guess not.'" Emma read the words, her throat catching. "Alexa J. is a local student who has requested her last name not be printed."

The phone clattered to the floor as Emma realized what this meant.

They weren't married yet. The pregnancy wasn't announced. If anything, the pregnancy would hurt Jackson and his company now. Not only was he cheating on Emma, he was cheating on a pregnant Emma.

There would be no salvaging his company's reputation after that. The board would kick him out and he wouldn't need Emma anymore. He wouldn't need her, or their child.

The contract wouldn't be valid anymore.

"That's why he didn't say he loved me back," she whispered, the full realization of it hitting her. "He doesn't. I fell for his act, hook, line and sinker. He played me."

Hot, angry tears splashed down her cheeks.

He didn't love her. He never had. She'd been played for a fool.

And now, she was useless to him. He would toss her out. Sure, she'd be able to get child support, but the love of her life would be gone.

She thought back to that night. He had come home that night, kissed her and cuddled with her for a moment. She didn't know he was kissing her with someone else's kisses. She didn't know that it was all a game to him.

If this had been some sort of accident, he hadn't mentioned it. He hadn't said a word about the other woman or the party, which made her think he was hiding it. He had deliberately not told her because he didn't want her to know he was cheating.

Now she knew. Now she knew that he didn't care and it shattered her.

The father of her child didn't want her anymore.

She didn't know that anything could hurt this much.

She'd felt heartbreak before, but never like this. Her heart ached not only for her, but for her unborn child. This betrayal affected both of them. She could never forgive him for this.

Emma sobbed into her hands. The perfect picture she had in her mind of the two of them raising a child together was gone. All of her hopes and dreams for the future were dashed to pieces now.

She wished she had never fallen in love with him. And it was her own fault for getting hurt like this. She knew what he was. She knew he was a player whose only usage of the word fidelity related to stocks and bonds.

She should have known she wouldn't be enough to keep him.

But she had hoped. She had let herself believe that he loved her. That he cared. That she had changed him and that they could walk away into a beautiful happily ever after.

But she was wrong. He didn't change. He couldn't. He wasn't capable of love or monogamy. It was his nature to want new women. He couldn't be happy with just one. He couldn't be content with a life with her. He would always need more.

Emma cried, burying her face in her arms. She wasn't enough.

Her phone continued to buzz and chime, telling her that she had an endless supply of emails and phone calls from various newspapers wanting to know how broken her heart was.

That gave her pause. How in the world did they get her number? It was supposed to be unlisted. Then she shook her head. It wouldn't be that hard to figure out. Anyone worth their salt could find a phone number, and her email wasn't exactly a secret. She couldn't blame them. A sound bite from the cheated on fiancee would be more than worth their effort.

She wiped at her face and felt the twist in her stomach. Just because she was crying and upset didn't stop her morning sickness from reminding her that it was there. She got up and finished making her ginger tea and ate a couple of crackers.

She chewed on the bland crackers and wondered if she might be overreacting. It was possible. She was pregnant and she could feel the hormones swirling around in her brain. She needed an outside opinion.

She picked her phone back up, ignoring the twenty-six text messages, seventy-two emails, and twenty-four phone calls. She dialed Grace.

"Emma! Are you okay?" Grace picked up on the second ring. "I just saw the picture."

"I don't know what to do," Emma admitted.

"You dump his ass is what you do," Grace told her. "He cheated on you, Emma. I don't care that he's a billionaire or how cute he is. That's a scum move. That's not someone you stick around with."

Emma deflated. She half hoped that Grace would tell her the photo was obviously photoshopped or that there must be a reason.

"Emma, do you have a place to go?" Grace asked. "You can come here if you need to. We have the guest room all set up. The baby crib is in there, but he doesn't like to sleep there."

"No, it's okay," Emma told her. "The apartment downstairs is in my name and paid for the year. He can't take it."

"Good. That was smart thinking."

Emma shook her head. "That was my lawyer's smart thinking. I'm an idiot."

"That's not true," Grace said sharply. "You saw the best in

him. You gave him a chance. It's not your fault that the guy couldn't keep it in his pants. That's not on you."

"Sure." Emma shrugged.

"Don't 'sure' me, Emma," Grace warned. "Do you remember the last guy who broke your heart? You remember what I did to him?"

Emma chuckled. "You egged his car. I had to take the baseball bat away from you."

"Damn straight. Chris saw the picture this morning and hid the bat, just so you know," Grace told her. "But, I know where the sporting goods store is. You tell me, and I'll buy two new ones."

"You're a good friend." Emma sighed. "I don't know what to do."

"You get out of his apartment. Take all your stuff out. Then, you don't talk to him. He's scum and he doesn't deserve someone as wonderful as you. He screwed up big time and you don't owe him anything."

Emma chewed on her lip. It wasn't that simple. She was carrying his child. She couldn't just shut him out. But, she hadn't told anyone about the pregnancy yet. Not even Grace.

"You listening, Emma?" Grace asked. "If you feel like you need to see him, you call me. I'll talk to him for you. You're my best friend and I don't like people messing with my friends."

Emma smiled a little bit. Her friend's fierce loyalty at least made her feel a little loved. Someone in the world cared about her.

"Okay, Grace. I'll do what you said," Emma replied.

"Okay. I'll be over in thirty minutes to help. I'm bringing some ice cream and animal crackers."

"Animal crackers?" Emma asked. That wasn't a usual breakup food.

"I have Sammy and it's all he wants to eat right now," Grace explained. "I figure he's good for cheering you up."

"I'd like to see him. See you soon."

Emma sighed and clicked off her phone. Everything felt hopeless. She pressed her hand to her stomach and closed her eyes.

"Don't you worry, little one," she promised the child growing in her belly. "I'll take care of you. Even if your father's awful, I've got you."

With that, she started to pack.

CHAPTER 32

Jackson

Jackson sat at his desk, head in his hands. He didn't know how to fix this one. He had screwed up. It wasn't really his fault, but now that it was happening, he could see a million different ways he could have prevented this.

'If onlys' whispered through his mind. He could have pushed the woman away sooner. He should have never been alone. He should have told Emma right away.

That was the one that hurt the most. He should have come straight home and told her that a strange woman had kissed him. She would have forgiven him then. She would have understood.

He sighed. Now it was too late. He'd kept the kiss to himself. For the first twenty-four hours, he thought he was safe. There were no news stories, no leaks. He had thought that it really was just an over-eager business student.

And then came the phone calls. Nearly the instant it hit the tabloids, he was deluged by phone calls.

Now there was a note from his housekeeper that Emma had moved all of her things out.

He ran his hands through his hair. How had this gotten out of control so quickly? He had barely seen the images himself before finding out that his fiancée had moved out. He couldn't blame her though.

He could only imagine what she must think of him. What she must be feeling. He was a notorious womanizer, and as far as she knew, he had just cheated on her in front of the entire world. If he were in her shoes, he would have left him too.

His office door flew open and hit the wall with a loud thud. Jane stood in the doorway, practically spitting fire. Her normally neat bun was a mess of gray streaks and her shirt was wrinkled.

"What the hell did you do?" she growled at him.

"I didn't do anything," he told her, trying to keep his calm.

"You didn't do anything?" Jane asked calmly, nodding her head as she spoke. "Then how the hell did they get that picture?"

"She kissed me. I was just standing there and she kissed me. I pushed her away."

"Right. Because the image I saw certainly looks like a man pushing away the woman with her tongue down his throat," Jane agreed sarcastically.

"I didn't kiss her," he growled back. "Do you really think I would do something so stupid?"

"Do you really want me to answer that?" Jane asked, putting her hands on her hips.

Jackson sighed. "I didn't kiss her. This was a setup. I called and told you that."

"You told me that there might be an issue. This is far

more than what you let on." Jane stomped over to his desk. She placed her hands on the smooth finish and leaned over the flat surface. "Look me in the eye and tell me that you didn't do this."

Jackson raised his gaze to meet hers. "I swear to you on my father's grave, I didn't kiss that woman. She kissed me and I pushed her away. This was not consensual."

Jane evaluated him for a moment, deciding if he was telling the truth.

"I wouldn't do this to Emma," Jackson said softly. He looked away from Jane and down at his hands. "I love her."

"I believe you," Jane said after a moment. She sighed and flopped into one of the chairs facing the desk. "The problem is, it's a good picture. It's very clearly you and the woman made it look hot and steamy."

"Emma moved out," Jackson said softly.

"When?" Jane asked, sitting up.

"Just now. The housekeeper messaged me." Jackson looked up. "I haven't had a chance to speak to her. She's not answering my calls."

"And you're sitting here because?" Jane asked, motioning to the room.

"I don't know what to do. I've never had to win back a girl." Jackson sighed. "I never cared to before."

"You realize she's the least of your problems, right?" Jane asked. "Your stock is plummeting. The board of directors is screaming for your head."

"Emma is my first priority," Jackson said firmly. He set his mouth. "She's pregnant."

"You have got to be kidding me." Jane pinched the bridge of her nose like she was getting a headache. Jackson certainly had one. "You just cheated on your pregnant fiancée?"

"I didn't cheat," Jackson growled.

"To the public, you did. They don't know it was staged," she replied. "This is bad. Does anyone else know?"

Jackson shook his head. "Just the doctors. We wanted to wait to announce it."

Jane pursed her lips. "The doctors can't legally tell anyone, so we're okay there. I'm glad one of you was thinking ahead. I'm guessing it was Emma."

Jackson nodded.

Jane rubbed her temples. "Tell me exactly how this happened. Maybe I can think of something."

"I went to a dinner party at the yacht club. Emma was supposed to attend, but she hasn't been feeling well. I went out on the balcony to call her. I spoke to her. Just as I finished with the call, this woman comes up claiming to be a student."

"And you didn't think that was odd?" Jane asked. "That a gorgeous woman has you alone?"

"Honestly? No." Jackson shrugged. "Two months ago, it *was* normal. Two months ago, I would have taken her home without a second thought. This has happened to me before, just with very different results."

"And she kissed you?"

Jackson nodded. "She made sure to turn me to the best light. And then she kissed me. I pushed her away, but the damage was done."

"It only takes a fraction of a second to take that photo," Jane agreed. She sighed. "It was the yacht club down on Vine and Sea-star?"

Jackson nodded.

Jane thought for a moment. "I might have an idea. If I do, it's only because I am amazing and you would owe me. Big."

For the first time all day, hope lit in Jackson's chest. "Really?"

"Don't get those big hopeful eyes just yet," she warned

him. "I'll look into it. You need to go salvage what you can with Emma. The fact that she moved out looks bad. It won't be long before Max figures that one out."

"You think Max did this?" Jackson asked. The name tasted sour on his tongue.

"Who else?" Jane laughed bitterly. "This is just his style. He set you up. He wants to destroy you."

Anger flashed red across Jackson's vision. Max was going to ruin not only his business, but Emma. Emma was the best thing Jackson had in this world and he wasn't going to tolerate it.

"Whoa, slow down there, Tiger," Jane warned. Jackson realized he was standing and halfway to the door. "You need to fix things with your girl. We need her on our side if you're going to survive any of this."

He stood there, at a loss. He'd never had to mend a broken heart before. He'd broken plenty of hearts, but he'd never wanted to save one. This was something completely new and foreign to him. He didn't even know where to start.

Jane sighed. "Bring her flowers. And jewelry. And if she has something expensive that she likes, bring her that, too," Jane advised. "You need to go to her on your knees. She's going to be furious with you."

"What do I say?" Jackson asked. "She's not going to want to listen to me."

"You apologize. You tell her the truth," Jane told him. She stood up and straightened his tie. "But most of all, you tell her you love her."

He looked down at Jane to see her smile sadly at him. "I really do," he said softly.

"I know." Jane nodded. "So get going."

∽

Jackson flew down the stairs. He sprinted across the lobby. He had his secretary calling ahead to have flowers and the biggest diamond necklace the jewelry shop had meet him at the apartment. He had to get to her. He had to make her see.

He couldn't lose her. Not like this.

He sprinted into the parking garage, ready to run every red light from here to the apartment.

"Wow, you're in a hurry," a snide voice said as he opened the parking structure door.

Jackson went cold and then hot with fury as he turned to face Max Singleton.

"You," Jackson snarled. He crossed the space between them in three big steps. He was going to punch the guy's lights out and then beat him to a bloody pulp.

"Whoa, whoa," Max said, holding up his hands and smiling. "Easy there, tiger." He pointed to a camera on a tripod facing him. "I'd hate for you to have yet more damning video evidence. It would be awful for you to punch an unarmed man for no reason."

"I have plenty of reason," Jackson replied. His fingers clenched, but he turned and started to walk away. "I don't have time for this."

"I have to say you trained her well," Max called out. Jackson stopped. "She only answered the phone once. Poor thing. She was so confused, but she managed to get out a 'no comment' before hanging up."

Jackson's hand balled into tight fists. He knew he should keep walking. He knew that Max was just goading him into doing something stupid. Something to keep up the charade that he was a bad boy with a womanizing attitude.

And it was all to sell diapers.

"You don't have proof this time," Max sneered. "There are no secret cameras. No surprise live videos. Just a picture of you passionately kissing another woman. And Alexa is so good at that. I win this time. I always win."

Jackson forced himself to start walking.

"Oh, did I mention that she's not a student?" Max asked, his voice bubbling with evil laughter. "She's a call girl. That'll come out this week. You cheated on your adorable, perfect, company-saving fiancée with a call girl. Poor, poor, sweet little Emma. You think I can get her number?"

"You don't get to talk about her," Jackson growled. The idea of Max hurting Emma more made his blood boil. He couldn't see straight. "You don't get to say her name."

"Careful," Max warned, pointing to the camera. "I'd hate for those mothers to see your bad side."

Jackson froze and the smiled. "You always were an idiot, Max."

"What?" Max looked confused. "I beat you. I've won."

Jackson went over, carefully standing out of frame and knocked the camera over. "Whoopsie," he said with a shrug.

Max paled.

Jackson then went and punched him square in the jaw.

It felt good.

"Too bad your camera broke," Jackson told him. He turned and walked away. He had to get to Emma before it was too late to fix things.

 *mma*

Emma didn't know it was possible to cry this much. She didn't know that she had this many tears inside of her. She didn't know that it was possible to feel this much pain from just one lie.

He kissed another woman.

He didn't love her.

She was obviously nothing to him.

She sat on her couch in her tiny apartment, mindlessly eating a pint of ice cream that she stole from his fridge, and cried.

The worst part was that she didn't even feel like she had the right to cry. It was in the contract that they could see other people. Their relationship was never meant to be about love. They were a business relationship. It was always supposed to be a way to keep the bad boy's business happy. She was only ever supposed to be the good girl image.

Yet, it still hurt. It hurt more than she ever thought possible.

He had cheated on her. Just because she had suspected this day might come didn't make it easier. When they had first started this arrangement, she thought she could handle it. She had thought she would be okay with knowing that he married her for money and not for love.

But then she fell for him. And, worse, she thought he had fallen for her too. She thought that he cared. Even though he never said the words, she thought that he loved her at least enough to give them a chance.

But, the photo proved that he was back to his old ways. She wasn't enough for him. Their child wasn't enough for him. He still needed more.

She wished she could quit the contract. She wished she could just disappear to another state and never see him again. But even that idea made her want to sob into her ice cream just as hard.

She loved him. Even after this, even after knowing that he didn't love her back, she still loved him. Perhaps that was the part that hurt the most. She was an idiot.

She wished she could dull the pain with wine. Or a full bottle of whiskey. Heartache wasn't nearly as bad when she could pass out and pretend it didn't exist.

But she wouldn't do that to her baby. Even if it was his. The baby was innocent in all of this. She wasn't sure how she would raise the child with the father being a total douche. It hurt even more that he would do this not only to her, but to their child. The man had no moral decency.

A soft knock on her door drew her attention. She checked her watch and saw that the food she'd ordered was due. She carefully set the half-eaten ice cream to the side and got up. She wasn't in the mood to see anyone but the pizza man tonight.

She went to the door and checked the peephole. The delivery guy was holding the pizza up to the door so she could see it. Smart man, she thought to herself. There was no way she was opening this door to anyone who didn't have her food. If a reporter wanted to talk to her, they would at least have to give her a pizza to do it.

She undid the lock and pulled the door open.

She promptly slammed it shut.

The pizza man wasn't there. It was Jackson, holding up the pizza. He must have caught the delivery guy on the way up and taken the pizza. Sneaky bastard.

"Go away," Emma yelled through the door. She was willing to give up her pizza not to have to see him. She had enough ice cream that she could make it through the night.

"Emma, please," Jackson called back. "I just want to explain."

Righteous fury lit up inside of her. What was there to explain? "No."

"Please, Emma," he begged. His voice was low and full of hurt. For a moment, Emma almost felt bad for him. Then she remembered that he was an expert in getting women to do what he wanted.

"Go away," she repeated.

"Emma, I didn't kiss her," he said through the door. "It was a set up."

She evaluated that statement for a moment. It could be true. She'd seen enough of the business world to know that people were willing to lie, cheat, and have babies for the company. It wouldn't be crazy to pay a woman to kiss him.

But that didn't change the fact that this caught her completely unprepared. He'd had a full two days to tell her. He'd kept it from her, hoping she'd never find out. He had lied by omission. It was just the first step down the path to him actually kissing another woman.

He didn't trust her. She told him everything, yet he thought it was okay to keep secrets like this from her. What kind of relationship could they have without trust?

She threw open the door, daggers shooting from her red, teary ears. "A set up?" She glared at him. "A strange woman kissed you, but you didn't think it was important to tell me. Thanks for the heads up."

She reached over, grabbed the pizza from his surprised hands, and slammed the door again.

"Emma!"

She put the pizza on the counter and locked the door. Her hands shook and tears ran down her face. She peeked through the peephole and saw him still standing there, his hand on the door like he was trying to reach out to her.

"Emma, I didn't think it was important," he said softly. "I didn't want to upset you."

"I think that turned out marvelously," Emma replied, still watching him. He winced.

"Can I please come in?" he asked again, looking around the hallway.

She chewed her bottom lip. She didn't want to see him, but she knew this needed to be done. They needed a conversation and shouting through the door wasn't the best way to do that. Who knew what the neighbors would tell the reporters.

She undid the lock and opened the door. "You have five minutes," she informed him. "Then you leave or I call the cops."

"Thank you," he said, stepping quickly inside.

She slammed the door behind him and crossed her arms. "Four minutes and thirty seconds," she reminded him. His shoulders slumped.

"Here, I brought you these," he said, holding out his hands. He had a bouquet of red roses and a large velvet box.

She assumed there was some kind of jewelry inside, but she didn't really care. She kept her arms crossed.

"Four minutes," she said coldly.

He set the box and the flowers down on the counter and ran his hand through his hair. The soft blond hair stuck up at funny angles.

"I'm sorry," he said.

"You should have led with that." She tapped her watch.

"I didn't kiss that woman," he told her. Her heart squeezed a little, but she wasn't about to let him know that. "It was a setup. I went out on the balcony to call you and she came to me. I told her I had to leave and she kissed me. I pushed her away, but the picture was already taken. Please, Emma. I didn't kiss her."

He looked at her, his beautiful green eyes pleading for her to understand.

And she did understand. She just wasn't ready to forgive him for this. The fact that he had kept this a secret hurt almost as much as him kissing someone else. It was still a betrayal.

"I believe you," she told him. Relief flooded his features and he took a step toward her, his arms outstretched. She moved away from him. "But I don't trust you."

"What?" A confused hurt filled his face that made her heart ache.

"You didn't tell me. You didn't tell me that a strange woman kissed you for no reason." Her voice felt cold. It hurt to talk after all the crying. "You kept this from me. I can't help you if you don't let me in. You don't trust me."

"But I do," he assured her. "Emma, I trust you more than anyone."

"You have a strange way of showing it," she remarked. Her chest felt like it was going to explode. She hated seeing him like this, but he had hurt her too badly. If she gave in and let this go, he would walk all over her for the rest of their relationship.

"Emma..."

"I will do whatever the contract requires," she informed him. "You don't have to worry about that. I will smile for the cameras, tell them all that I forgive you and it was a simple mistake. I will hold your hand in public and tell everyone what an amazing father you are. I won't reveal our contract or act out in spite. But I won't ever trust you again."

"What do you mean?" His voice caught at the end of the question, implying that he knew what she meant.

"As far as the public is concerned, we are a happy, loving couple." Her voice shook on the word loving. "But we are done. I can't trust you and you obviously don't trust me. It's not the kiss that did this. It was you."

"Emma, please don't do this," he begged. "Please. I love you."

"You love me?" Anger flared again. "You tell me that now? You only say it when it gets you something. I don't believe you."

"It's the truth, Emma," he told her, his eyes shining.

She wanted to believe him. She wanted to have him wrap his arms around her and tell her that everything was fine now. She wanted him to kiss her and make her feel special again.

And she would be fine. Until this happened again. Until he decided not to tell her that someone kissed him. Or worse, that he kissed someone. Given his nature, it was only a matter of time before he grew bored with her.

She didn't want to go through this a second time. Better to stay firm now and not get hurt by him a second time.

"Your time's up," she whispered. "You need to leave now."

"Emma, please. I love you. Please believe me." His tone bordered on frantic and it tore at her heart. She held firm.

"Please leave, Jackson," she said, pointing to the door. "If you need me to do anything, have your secretary contact me. Or Jane. I don't want to talk to you anymore."

She walked over and opened the door to the apartment, holding it open for him to leave.

He stood in her kitchen for a moment, completely lost.

"What can I do?" he asked. "What can I do to fix this? What do I need to say?"

Emma looked up at him, hardening her heart. "That was something you should have said yesterday. Today is too late. You're too late."

He closed his eyes and nodded. His steps from the apartment were slow and measured, as if he were forcing himself to move and using every inch of his willpower to do it. He stepped out into the hallway.

"I'm sorry, Emma."

She couldn't think of another time she'd ever heard him apologize. He was the billionaire CEO of one of the biggest corporations in the US. He didn't have to apologize to anyone, but he was apologizing to her.

She didn't care. It was too little too late.

She closed the door and walked away.

ackson

Jackson went back up to his apartment, got in the shower, and cried.

He hadn't cried since he was five years old and his pet turtle died. He hadn't cried like this when his parents died. He didn't know that it was possible for a grown man to feel this much hurt inside.

He had screwed up. Big time.

Why hadn't he just told her? He could have come home from the party and told her then. He could have mentioned it the next day. It would have been so easy.

He wanted to say it was to protect her. He wanted to believe it was because he was keeping her calm for the baby.

But that was a lie.

He was doing it to protect himself. He was afraid she would leave him. That she wouldn't smile up at him like he was the best thing in the world. That she wouldn't tease him or make him laugh because she would finally see his true nature.

And he had made it a self-fulfilling prophecy. By not telling her, he had ruined things. He had broken their trust.

He should have told her that he loved her the moment he knew. She deserved love. He didn't need to wait and make a spectacle out of it. Their whole lives were a spectacle. Their love didn't need to be.

But, he had waited to make himself look better. He had kept the kiss to himself to make himself look better.

It had only made him look worse.

A slow resolve started to form, deep in his core. It took hold, growing like a chain of iron, link by link until he was full of strength.

He would prove himself. He would win her back. He would show her that he was the kind of man she deserved.

He would make this right.

He turned off the water and got to work.

"You must be the luckiest son of a bitch I've ever met," Jane said, walking into his office the next day.

He'd spent the night trying to think of a way to make things right with Emma. He hadn't come up with anything that felt right, so now he was out of ideas, exhausted, and cranky.

"What do you want, Jane?" Jackson snapped at his PR adviser. She really needed to learn how to knock and not just waltz into his office.

"Is that any way to speak to the woman about to save your company and possibly even your relationship?" Jane asked, crossing her arms. A cocky smile crossed her lips.

"If you can do that, then I'll change my tone," he replied. He wanted another cup of coffee, but coffee always made him think of Emma.

Jane grinned. "Then change your tone and smile, Jackson. I've got your saving grace."

"Spit it out," he said, not changing his sharp tone. "Nobody likes a tease."

Jane put a thumb drive on his desk.

"Let me just turn into a computer and magically read what's on that," Jackson said, looking at the drive. He didn't bother to pick it up.

"Well, aren't you in a pleasant mood," Jane commented. She sat down on her favorite chair and grinned. "It's you obviously pushing the girl away. In video."

Jackson's breath caught. "How? I thought the club's security cameras were off. You said Max was thorough this time."

"He was. I'm just better than he is," she replied casually. "That's why you hired me."

Jackson picked up the small silver thumb drive, hope forming for the first time in days. "Where did you get it?"

Jane grinned. "The dock holds some of the most expensive yachts in the world. You don't think they have their own security cameras?"

Jackson looked up at her.

"I deserve a bonus for this by the way. I had to contact fifty yacht owners, convince them to let me look at their security footage that wasn't mysteriously missing, and then go through all of it." She pointed to the thumb drive. "I haven't slept, and all so I could get you that little one minute and twenty-three seconds of tape."

"I could kiss you," Jackson said, feeling a smile cross his face.

"Please don't. That's how we got into this mess," Jane

teased. She sighed. "And just so you know, you now owe the CEO of some publishing company a large favor."

He held the thumb drive in his palm, knowing that at least his public approval could be gained back by what was on it. "Worth it. How did Max not find it?"

"It wasn't a yacht. It was a little sailboat off to the side that got put in the yacht dock area because they overbooked. I had to look at the dock records to find it. But mostly, it's because I don't forget the little guy like he does. Max must not have thought the guy was important."

"Whatever your publishing guy wants, it's his. And you. You want a summer house in Paris? An island? It's yours."

"I like the way you think," Jane replied with a laugh. "Just a bonus is enough. And, I want a photo of Max's face at the press conference where you show the world this."

"I'll hire a photographer and have it put on an eight-by-ten canvas for your wall," he promised.

Jane's nose crinkled in disgust. "Ugh, no. I mean, it's going to be an amazing look for him, but I don't want to see his face in any shape on my wall."

Jackson nodded. "Press conference is what time?"

"Two o'clock, downstairs," Jane replied. "I have a speech written out for you. You'll say how hurt you are by these accusations and that you would never, ever do this willingly to Emma." Jane paused and looked at him. "If you can have Emma there, that would be helpful."

He sighed and ran his fingers through his hair. "She'll do it if you call her," he said. "She isn't speaking to me right now."

"She knows it was fake, right?" Jane asked. "Why is she angry?"

"Because I didn't tell her it happened in the first place. She found out when everybody else did," he explained. "She's not mad about the kiss. She's mad that I kept it from her. And she's got every right to be."

"Oh, Jackson." Jane shook her head. "That was stupid."

"No kidding," he agreed. The hopeful feeling left his chest. Without Emma in his life, nothing felt worth it. "I was trying to protect her and it backfired."

"She doesn't have to be at the press conference," Jane said gently. "It's really more about you, anyway. I can make the optics of it work."

Jackson looked down at the thumb drive sitting on his desk. There was a solution here. He could feel it. There was a way to make this better. It was going to cost him some pride, but Emma was worth anything.

"I want to add some things to the speech." Jackson looked up at Jane. "And I'd like you to make sure she's there. I need her there."

"Oh. You're going to go down the full honesty path, huh?" Jane thought for a second then nodded. "It's risky, but it could work out well for the company." She looked at him. "If what you're thinking of doing doesn't work, you know it will ruin everything, right? If she doesn't take you back, I can't repair the damage. There's no way you can keep the image you need."

Jackson nodded. "I'm willing to risk it. For her."

Jane sighed. "You really do love her, don't you?"

"With everything I've got," he replied, his voice firm. "So you'll help?"

"Yeah. I'm a sucker for a good love story," Jane replied with a laugh. "It's a good thing I like you. And her. Otherwise, the risk of you destroying all my hard work *again* would be too much."

She got up and turned to leave the office.

"Don't you need this?" Jackson asked, holding out the thumb-drive

"You think that's the only copy?" Jane scoffed. "I have that sucker uploaded on three cloud devices. I've worked too hard to let you screw everything up."

Jackson chuckled. "Thank you, Jane."

"Let's just hope she forgives you," she replied. "Or it won't matter how many cloud devices I have."

CHAPTER 35

Emma stood off the side of the small area Jane had designated as "the stage," hiding in a shadowy corner. There were several cameras already set up and several reporters checking their mics and making sure the lighting was good.

She just wanted to go home. The last thing Emma had wanted to do today was put on a pretty dress, do her hair and makeup, and come down to Jackson's office. Especially since he was the last person in the world she wanted to see.

But, Jane had invoked the contract. Emma had to be here.

Emma fussed with her necklace, making sure to stay out of sight of the reporters. She wasn't sure what was going on, but since her contract required it, she was here. She had a feeling Jackson was going to come out, address the picture as a fake, and have her stand next to him and smile.

She would do it, too. As a woman, she was well-versed in giving fake smiles. She could pretend that this didn't hurt her down to the core of her soul. She would smile and wave and no one would know that her heart was breaking.

"You look perfect," Jane said, coming up from the side. Jane wore a smart gray pantsuit that flattered her lean figure and matched her hair. She wore a headset and had a tablet and phone in each hand.

"Thank you," Emma said politely. "Where do you need me?"

"For right now, over here is perfect," Jane replied. She scrolled through something on the tablet. "Jackson will be out in just a moment and then I'll have you get into place."

"Do you need me to stand on the stage?" Emma asked. She set her shoulders. She could do this.

"No, that's not necessary," Jane told her. "I actually want the cameras to focus on Jackson for the most part."

"Really?" Emma was surprised. She was sure Jane would want the loving fiancée standing faithfully next to the accused.

Jane looked up from the tablet. "Yes."

Emma waited for more, but Jane just went back to her tablet.

"Okay, then." Emma rocked back on her heels and waited. Jane gave her a polite smile, and then went to yell at a photographer that was crossing some boundary for the cameras.

"Emma? This way please," Jane called to her after a moment. Emma hurried to the older woman's side as they walked away from the stage.

"Where are we going?" Emma asked. This wasn't what she was expecting at all.

"I'd like you to sit here please," Jane instructed, motioning to a chair marked with a "Reserved" sign. It was well behind the camera line and far away from the stage. She wasn't going to be on camera at all sitting back here.

"Sure." Emma took her seat and carefully folded her hands in her lap.

Well, this was a waste of makeup, she thought to herself. *Why am I even here?*

A photographer turned and snapped her picture. Emma just shrugged. Maybe the makeup wasn't a complete waste.

There was a bustle of activity from the cameras just before Jackson walked out on stage. Even though she was still angry and hurt by him, he took her breath away.

He stood tall in a dark blue suit and a rich burgundy tie. The coloring brought out the green of his eyes and the soft golds in his hair. He looked like a modern day prince.

Walking confidently up to the microphone, there was no way to tell that he wasn't in complete control. Only Emma saw the hunch in his shoulders, the tightness in his jaw, and the guarded smile. He was nervous.

For good reason, she thought. If the local gossips were to be believed, all security footage from the yacht club had mysteriously gone missing. Many of the docked yachts had their cameras turned the wrong way, or even off for the evening. There was no one to refute his story that the kiss wasn't consensual.

He was about to stand in front of a bunch of reporters and tell them that although he had no proof that he hadn't done this thing. She wondered again why she wasn't up on the stage with him, or at least closer to the stage.

Jackson's eyes scanned the crowd, coming to rest on her. She felt the familiar shiver of desire when he looked at her, even from across the room. When he looked at her like that, she was the only person in the entire world. She was the only living creature that mattered.

His mouth twitched like he wanted to smile at her. She raised her hand and tried to appear like this wasn't breaking her heart. If anyone was looking, they would think she was here for moral support and that nothing was wrong.

"Thank you, ladies and gentlemen for joining me today. First, I'd like to address the vicious rumors going around that I am involved with a woman other than my fiancée. I want to state expressly that this is a bald-faced lie." He paused and smiled around the room. "And I have proof."

Emma couldn't help but gasp. So did several reporters.

"If you'll please turn your attention to the screen here," Jackson said, motioning to a flat screen TV near him. He clicked a small button and the screen came to life. "This is security footage from a small sailboat in the dock. It was overlooked at first, but as with many good things, it warranted a second look."

Emma wondered if he meant something more by that statement, but didn't have time to ponder it as the security footage began to roll.

Everything was black and white, but the balcony of the yacht club was easily visible. The man talking on his phone was clearly Jackson. She could even see the soft smile as he spoke before hanging up the phone.

Every eye in there watched as a woman approached him. He took a step back. She came forward. He retreated further. She grabbed his arm, and he visibly stiffened. Up on stage, Emma could see Jackson stiffen along with his video counterpart.

Video Jackson pulled away, clearly turning to leave. The woman reached up, forcing a kiss that lastly hardly seconds before Jackson clearly pushed her away. It was obvious he was angry as he stormed inside.

The film clip ended, freezing on the woman looking out of the balcony and giving a thumbs up sign.

Emma had believed him when he said he didn't kiss the woman, but some part of her had wondered. He was known for his love of women and not caring if they were in a relationship or not. To see it on screen, clearly showing that everything he had told her was true, made it finally feel real.

"As you can see, the picture doesn't tell the whole story," Jackson said, into the microphone.

Emma was glad. He was safe again. He could keep his new image and the company would be successful because of it. She would play her part, even if it broke her.

It was still too little, too late for their relationship. He should have told her what happened that night. She would never have blamed him for this. She would have helped him fight it. But, he didn't. He chose to keep this from her, and that was why she was angry.

She couldn't trust him if he kept things from her. If he kept this to himself, what other things was he hiding? She couldn't afford the pain.

"I want to make something very, very clear here," Jackson continued. His eyes now went directly to Emma. "I love my fiancée."

She didn't move. This she expected.

"I didn't tell her when it first happened," Jackson continued. "You see, Emma is the kindest, gentlest, and best soul I've ever met. I was afraid to tell her that my past history had caught up to me. I was embarrassed, because I didn't feel I deserved her. Especially after all the things I've done. I will never keep anything from her, ever again."

The reporters were suddenly very quiet. Emma felt like a small spotlight was on her, but she didn't dare look away from Jackson's eyes. This was something special. He was putting himself out there, publicly for her.

"I want to take this opportunity, to publicly tell her that I'm sorry. That I don't deserve someone as amazing as Emma in my life. That she's more than I ever could have hoped and dreamed of. She's my everything." His voice shook slightly. "I love you, Emma."

Emma's breath came in short pants as her body forgot how to breathe properly. But, he wasn't done yet.

"Emma, I want you to know that what we have is worth more than anything to me." He swallowed. "I want to rip up our contract and just have it be us."

Emma's heart lurched and the stopped in her chest. It was a good thing she was sitting down, because she felt her legs turn to jelly. This was more than just an apology. Going in front of the world and telling every single person that he had failed was more than she expected. It was the ultimate form of apology for him.

She felt more than saw the cameras turn to her. Many of them had looks of confusion on their faces, but she didn't notice. The only thing she saw know was Jackson.

"I want us to be a real family," Jackson continued. "I want you to know that I choose you not because I have to, but because I want to. Because I love you."

He took a step closer to her.

"And I tell you this now, here, so that the whole world can know." He smiled at her. "I want every man on Earth to know that you're mine."

A tear trickled down her cheek. "Jackson," she whispered.

"Please be mine," he said, his voice catching at the end with emotion.

The entire audience held their breath, waiting for her to respond. She looked up at the stage, seeing only his beautiful green eyes. He loved her and now the whole world knew it.

He wanted it to be real. He wanted their relationship to be more than just a contract. He was visibly nervous. He was afraid she would say no to him. He didn't have control this time.

"Yes," she whispered. This was a real proposal. This was

what love looked like. It wasn't fancy fireworks and diamond rings. It was promises and honesty. It was understanding and compromise.

She stood slowly to her feet. She wasn't quite sure how she got to the stage, but suddenly she was standing across from him with only a few feet between them. The reporters and the stage disappeared from her mind.

"I can't promise to be perfect," he whispered. "But, I want this to be real."

"Okay."

His smile illuminated her entire world. It was everything. She fell into his arms and he kissed her. Joy and hope crashed through her, followed by bliss. This was real. This wasn't just a charade they were putting on for others. It wasn't something to sell diapers.

It was real. It was love.

"We're home, little one," Emma whispered, standing on the front step of their home. A light snow started to fall, coating the world in perfect serenity.

"I've got her," Jackson said, taking the car seat from Emma's hands and carrying their daughter inside. He smiled first at Emma, and then cooed at their daughter as he brought her in.

Emma smiled after them and slowly made her way inside. They were home.

A fire crackled in the fireplace for their arrival. Emma loved this house. It was just a few miles outside of the city, but it felt like they were in their own private world out here. It was the perfect place to raise a family.

"Welcome home, Hope," Jackson whispered, taking his tiny daughter out of the car seat. She looked so tiny in his arms, yet perfectly safe. She still couldn't believe the hospital had let them take her home. She was so precious.

The little girl yawned and snuggled into her father. Jackson nearly glowed with pride as he smiled at her.

Children suited him.

"Come sit with us, Emma," he whispered.

"You just don't want to set her down," Emma teased, joining him on the couch.

"Why would I?" he asked, gazing down adoringly. "She's perfect."

"She is," Emma agreed.

Jackson looked up, his green eyes going to hers. "You're perfect," he told her. His eyes said he meant it.

She leaned over and kissed him.

This was how life was supposed to be, she thought. A loving husband. A beautiful child. A warm home.

This was all she'd ever wanted. It was strange to think that she'd started it all with a contract. Jackson hadn't been kidding when he said he was going to rip it up. He did the night of the press conference, the lawyers be damned.

And the next day, he'd flown her out to the mountains and married her.

For real.

It was all for real now. There was no fake relationship. There were no legal loopholes or ways to sneak out of obligations.

For better or for worse, Jackson and Emma were in this together. Only now, they had a beautiful baby girl to make things even better.

"I'm so happy," Jackson whispered, his eyes on his newborn daughter. He looked up at Emma with tears of joy. "So happy."

Emma didn't have the words. There were no words in the human language to describe the beautiful joy she felt.

So she kissed her husband.

Hey there! I'm so happy you enjoyed this book about the billionaire and the barista. There are two other books of mine coming out this month, and I'd like to share a little from each of them with you. Read on!

FAMILY DOCTOR'S BABY

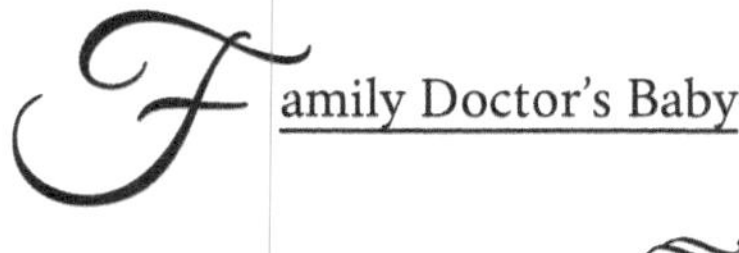

amily Doctor's Baby

~

From New York Times bestselling author Krista Lakes, comes a sexy standalone novel about the baddest bad boy doctor and the sweet little nurse that he falls for.

When I left my small hometown years ago, I never expected to come back. I certainly never expected that when I did, I'd be working for *him*.

He's the town's doctor. He's supposed to be a respectable member of society, a pillar for the community. He's supposed to have come a long way from the bad boy who rode a motorcycle in high school.

But he hasn't. One glance from those lustful eyes looking at me tells me that he has the same voracious appetites that he did when we were younger.

Only it's not quite the same stare. It's more urgent. It's more intense. I'm not the same nerdy girl who tutored him.

I've grown up, developed fertile curves that I know he finds irresistible.

In this small town, rumors travel fast, and the family doctor can't be seen as a player. So he does try to resist. And I do too. But with every smoldering glance and moment of sexual tension, we find our barriers breaking down.

After a stressful night of touch-and-go baby delivery, a moment of elation overcomes our inhibitions. It seems like maybe we'll need to confront those rumors sooner rather than later, especially before I begin to show the results of that night.

Can I give this doctor the family he has always desired?

Dr. Matthews leaned in and brought his lips toward mine. He paused right before our lips touched. Just for a moment, though. It was as if he were making sure that I wanted this. The universe held its breath as we both held our breath. I noticed everything from the way his aftershave lingered in the air to the water droplets in his hair. After a second that felt like eternity, he leaned in the rest of the way, firmly pressing his lips against mine.

Our fate was sealed.

A soft moan made its way up my throat as I relaxed into his kiss. I closed my eyes and let my hands drift up toward his face. His beard stubble tickled my fingertips as I dragged them over his cheeks.

It must have been the adrenaline we'd both experienced that morning. Or maybe it was that the emergency had bonded us closer than ever before. I didn't know what had gotten into either of us, but I suppose it didn't need explaining. It felt good and right and that's all I really cared about. I needed a release that only he could give me.

Jacob slowly broke our kiss and dropped his hands to the top of my hips. Then he leaned in again, passionately pressing his lips to mine. My heart began to do flip flops behind my rib cage. Within a few seconds, I felt Jacob open his mouth and gently dart his tongue out, teasing it into my mouth.

A tingling sensation coursed through my body as our tongues lightly wrestled with each others, twisting around in a sensual dance. I reveled in the sensations: his taste, his smell, the way he held his body against mine. This wasn't a dream. This was actually happening.

Jacob broke the kiss and took a step back. His cheeks were flushed and his eyes dark.

"I'm sorry. That was unprofessional."

My heart hammered in my chest and my lips ached for more of his kisses.

"I don't care," I told him. "I don't want to stop."

He looked up, his eyes bright as they met mine. Desire that matched my own shone in them and my body heated. I took the step forward to bring us back together. Slowly, I brought my hand up and wrapped it around the back of his neck.

"Are you sure you're okay with this?" he asked, his hands already coming to my hips.

"Just shut up and kiss me," I said, still smiling.

<u>Family Doctor's Baby</u>

rime Boss Baby

From New York Times bestselling author Krista Lakes, comes a sensual, standalone mafia romance that will have you turning the pages at record speed.

I am a mafia princess.

My family is making me marry a rival crime boss.

At first, I go along with it because it's important to my family. But then I meet *him*.

Dante is dangerous and sexy as sin. I want him physically and mentally. His talented fingers and mouth have me panting for more before he even knows my real name.

But there are parts of my past that can ruin everything. My mother's murderer is catching up to me. If he finds me, he could ruin everything. Not only that, not everyone in Dante's family is as excited about the wedding as they appear.

And then, there's news that both overjoys and terrifies me. I'm pregnant.

Can Dante save me and give me the future we both desire? Or will my past destroy everything and everyone that I care about?

ABOUT THE AUTHOR

New York Times and USA Today Bestseller Krista Lakes is a thirtysomething who recently rediscovered her passion for writing. She is living happily ever after with her Prince Charming. Her first kid just started preschool and she is happy to welcome her second child into her life, continuing her "Happily Ever After"!

Thank you for supporting an indie author. Anything you can do, whether it be writing a review, or even simply telling a fellow reader that you enjoyed this, helps me out immensely. Thanks!

Krista would love to hear from you! Please contact her at Krista.Lakes@gmail.com or friend her on Facebook!

Further reading:

Bad Boys and Babies
  Family Doctor's Baby
  The Billionaire's Baby Arrangement
  Crime Boss Baby

Kinds of Love
  A Forever Kind of Love
  A Wonderful Kind of Love

An Endless Kind of Love

Billionaires and Brides
Yours Completely: A Cinderella Love Story
Yours Truly: A Cinderella Love Story
Yours Royally: A Cinderella Love Story

The "Kisses" series
Saltwater Kisses: A Billionaire Love Story
Kisses From Jack: The Other Side of Saltwater Kisses
Rainwater Kisses: A Billionaire Love Story
Champagne Kisses: A Timeless Love Story
Freshwater Kisses: A Billionaire Love Story
Sandcastle Kisses: A Billionaire Love Story
Hurricane Kisses: A Billionaire Love Story
Barefoot Kisses: A Billionaire Love Story
Sunrise Kisses: A Billionaire Love Story
Waterfall Kisses: A Billionaire Love Story
Island Kisses: A Billionaire Love Story

Other Novels
I Choose You: A Secret Billionaire Romance
His Every Desire: A Billionaire Seduction
Wolf Six's Salvation: A Shifter Love Story
Burned: A New Adult Love Story
Walking on Sunshine: A Sweet Summer Romance
An American Cinderella: A Royal Love Story
Mr. Darcy's Kiss: A Contemporary Pride and Prejudice